Karate Masters

"Hey, Mr. Miyagi, look!" Daniel called, halting his friend and pointing to the ad. From high above them on the poster the menacing features of Mr. Miyagi's old rival, Sato, glared in icy fury. His right hand was smashing through twelve one-inch wooden boards, sending splinters of wood exploding outward from the blow. Beneath the photograph were the words:

LEARN KARATE FROM MASTER SATO
AT OKINAWA'S BIGGEST DOJO
FORTY YEARS OFFICAL INSTRUCTOR
TO THE U.S. MILITARY
PROVEN IN COMBAT

"Isn't that the guy you were telling me about?" Daniel asked in awe.

"*Hai*," he answered frowning.

"Can *you* break wood like that?"

Mr. Miyagi sniffed in disdain. "Don't know," he answered. "Never been attacked by tree."

COLUMBIA PICTURES Presents

A JERRY WEINTRAUB PRODUCTION A JOHN G. AVILDSEN FILM

RALPH MACCHIO NORIYUKI "PAT" MORITA

THE KARATE KID

PART II

Music by BILL CONTI Music Supervisor BROOKS ARTHUR Production Designed by WILLIAM J. CASSIDY

Director of Photography JAMES CRABE Executive Producer R.J. LOUIS Written by ROBERT MARK KAMEN

Based on Characters Created by ROBERT MARK KAMEN Produced by JERRY WEINTRAUB

READ THE SCHOLASTIC BOOK Directed by JOHN G. AVILDSEN

The Karate Kid II
Part

A novelization by B.B. Hiller. Based on the
motion picture written by Robert Mark Kamen.
Based on characters created by Robert Mark Kamen.

SCHOLASTIC INC.
New York Toronto London Auckland Sydney

for Emmons B.

ISBN 0-590-40292-7

12 11 10 9 8 7 6 5 4   6 7 8 9/8 0 1/9

Printed in the U. S. A.   01

The Karate Kid Part II

Prologue

Daniel LaRusso had never felt better in his life. Sure, his knee hurt. He could barely put any weight on it, but it would heal in time. His rib hurt, too, but that would get better as well.

Champion. He said the word to himself, then out loud to the institutional gray tiles of the shower room. "Champion of the All-Valley Under 18 Karate Tournament." He liked the sound of that, even under the rush of water in the shower.

He took the soap and began to wash himself, gingerly, avoiding the bruises he'd acquired on his way to the championship during the tournament.

The tournament had been the culmination of months of demanding karate training by his *sensei* — his teacher and friend, Mr. Miyagi, a man who always had a way of surprising Daniel. It was Mr. Miyagi who had guided him wisely through his training, showing him that in karate, his worst enemy could be himself. Daniel had learned that the best reason to become good at karate was so that he wouldn't have to fight.

Fighting was the last answer to every problem.

When Daniel had first moved to California from New Jersey, he'd gotten into a fight with Johnny Lawrence over a pretty girl named Ali Mills. That fight had led to another and another until Mr. Miyagi, the handyman in Daniel's shabby apartment complex, had stepped in, saving Daniel's life. Mr. Miyagi began to teach Daniel the lessons about karate that he had learned fifty years earlier from his father in Okinawa, and that Johnny would never learn from his own *sensei*, a man named Kreese. Kreese had taught Johnny that winning was everything, no matter how or why. Mr. Miyagi had taught Daniel better.

"Ouch!" Daniel said aloud. His wandering thoughts had made him forget his injured knee momentarily and he'd rubbed it vigorously with the washcloth. That brought his mind back to the tournament. He was still bursting with pride at his success. He could still hear the crowd yelling. He could still feel the excitement. Champion.

"Hey, Mr. Miyagi, I was thinking —"

"About what, Daniel-*san*?" Mr. Miyagi asked, standing outside the shower, waiting patiently with a towel.

"That maybe we should have a strategy now."

"For what?"

"My tournament career."

"Miyagi already has one."

Daniel shelved the soap and turned off the water. Peering around the shower curtain, he reached for the towel. Eagerly, he asked, "Yeah? What's our strategy?"

"Early retirement," Mr. Miyagi said in calm

certainty, tossing Daniel the towel and leaving him to dry himself, and think.

Ten minutes later, Daniel and Mr. Miyagi emerged from the locker room to find a group of young fans waiting for Daniel, asking him for autographs. A little embarrassed, Daniel obliged them, handing the large championship trophy to Ali, who had joined them. As Daniel signed his name, one of the referees stepped over to him to congratulate him as well.

"Very impressive win, son. You showed a lot of poise under pressure."

"Thank you," Daniel said.

"People will be talking about that last kick for years —"

He was cut off by the slam of the door behind him. Kreese came stalking out, pushing his way through the lingering crowd, his face frozen in a scowl. He paused near Daniel and Mr. Miyagi, almost as if to speak, but he only glowered at them in fury. Mr. Miyagi stared back at him evenly. Angrier still, Kreese stormed off to the parking lot.

In a way, Daniel understood it. Kreese had staked his whole reputation on the match between Daniel and Johnny. Kreese had even had one of his students try to disable Daniel in a preliminary match so that he wouldn't even be able to compete with Johnny. The stinging in Daniel's knee would remind him for a long time to come just exactly how close Kreese had come to succeeding in that. When Johnny had failed to beat Daniel, Kreese lost, too. But Johnny had learned something. Kreese hadn't. Daniel shook his head, watching Kreese's back.

"Why does he act like that?" he said to no one in particular.

"He doesn't know any better," the referee answered. That answer made Kreese sound like a child, a spoiled child — but a dangerous one.

"He should learn," Daniel said.

"You want to be the one to teach him?" the referee asked, without expecting an answer. He smiled. "Good luck, and again, congratulations."

"Thanks."

"Ready?" Mr. Miyagi asked.

"Sure, just a second," Daniel answered, signing two final autographs. He took the trophy out of Ali's hands and they followed Mr. Miyagi toward the parking lot. The trio had some celebrating to do.

As they rounded the building, though, they were surprised to come upon Kreese talking to Johnny. The two of them stood near Kreese's van. Johnny, with his second place trophy strapped to his dirt bike, had been just about to leave. The other students from Kreese's *dojo* gaped at the way Kreese was yelling at Johnny. In fact, Kreese held him by the shirt and was snarling with fury.

"I had him crippled for you and you still couldn't beat him!"

"It wasn't my fault," Johnny answered.

"You implying it was *mine*?"

From the side, Mr. Miyagi spoke.

"Why you no pick on someone your own size?"

"Mind your own business, old man."

"Who you calling old man, monkey face?"

Kreese met the challenge by shoving Johnny aside like a rag doll. The vicious *sensei* rushed Mr. Miyagi with a lunge, punching at his face. With a sinking heart, Daniel realized there was no referee here, nobody to keep it clean.

Kreese's fist was fast, but not fast enough. Mr. Miyagi calmly sidestepped the punch and it landed on the windshield of the van behind him, creating a spider web pattern around Kreese's bruised fist. Enraged, Kreese lunged again. This time, Mr. Miyagi did not sidestep. At the last possible moment, he raised his hand, palm out, and intercepted Kreese's fist. Kreese stopped dead in his tracks. A cold smile seemed to touch the corners of Mr. Miyagi's mouth as he slowly applied pressure to Kreese's fist, forcing him to the ground.

Kreese was on his knees, held frozen by Mr. Miyagi's left hand. Daniel was proud of his teacher and of the evident awe Kreese's students showed for Mr. Miyagi.

But then, to Daniel's horror, Mr. Miyagi brought back his powerful right hand, cocked for action, and spoke. It was Mr. Miyagi's voice, but these were not his words.

"Mercy is for the weak. We do not train to be merciful. A man faces you. He is the enemy. An enemy deserves no mercy."

These were the words Daniel and Mr. Miyagi had heard Kreese speak to his students. Daniel looked at Mr. Miyagi in surprise, but the old man's face was a mask of vengeance.

No. This could *not* be Mr. Miyagi. This was not the man who had taught him. No. Daniel could not believe what he was seeing.

He glanced at Kreese's students, frightened at the strength of the old man's apparent hatred, sure of the revenge it would serve on their *sensei*. Then Daniel looked at Kreese, the man of ice, melted by fear.

Mr. Miyagi's eyes flashed. His cocked hand sailed through the air, whistling toward Kreese's unprotected head.

Daniel closed his eyes. Then looked.

The chop had stopped with the same power that propelled it, less than an inch from Kreese's nose. A minute passed. Then Mr. Miyagi's forefinger flicked out and nubbed Kreese's nose in the lowest form of insult.

Briefly, Mr. Miyagi looked to Daniel and winked. A feeling of relief rushed through Daniel as he watched him step away from Kreese. Daniel ran to Mr. Miyagi — his friend, his teacher — and embraced him, filled with pride and happiness. With his other arm he reached for Ali, and together the three friends walked to Mr. Miyagi's pickup truck.

Daniel paused to look over his shoulder at Kreese and his students. One by one, he saw the students take off their belts and drop them in front of the still kneeling Kreese. One by one, they walked away from him, away from his teaching. At last they, too, had learned from Mr. Miyagi.

They had learned that the secret to karate lies in the mind and heart. Not in the fist.

Chapter 1

Daniel slammed his foot into the clutch pedal and downshifted, as he turned onto the dirt road that led to Mr. Miyagi's house. He needed to downshift; he didn't need to do it as angrily as he did.

It had been six months since he'd won the karate championship. He'd had many good times since then, but now it seemed as if they had all been erased by the last twenty-four hours, culminating in last night's prom. The prom was supposed to be the highlight of the year. Some highlight.

He pulled the car to a stop and turned off the engine, shaking his head slowly. Disgusted, he stepped down to survey the dent in the left front fender, leaving his crumpled tuxedo jacket on the front seat, next to his clip-on bow tie and Ali's abandoned corsage.

Mr. Miyagi emerged from his house.

"Daniel-*san*, must have been some prom. What happened?"

"What didn't happen is more like it. First, Ali redesigned my fender. Then she tells me she's fallen in love with some football player from U.C.L.A."

Mr. Miyagi was philosophical. "Things could be worse," he offered.

"They are," Daniel informed him. "Last night my mom got picked for a two-month management training course by her supervisor. We leave tomorrow night. For Fresno. I can't believe I'm going to spend my summer in *Fresno*." He kicked at the tire for emphasis, but only succeeded in bruising his toe on the hubcap.

Mr. Miyagi grunted in acknowledgment while he felt around under the dented fender. He had given Daniel this car — a yellow 1950 Chevrolet convertible — and he'd conditioned it before that, so he knew every inch of it.

"Think you can fix it?" Daniel asked.

Mr. Miyagi did not answer. Instead, he concentrated on the fender, solemnly examining the dent by feeling it with his fingers. Then, with his left hand pressed upward in the wheel well, he delivered a fast karate chop with the edge of his right hand to the side of the dent. Daniel watched as the metal obediently popped back into place, as good as new. He shook his head in amazement.

Mr. Miyagi stood up and took Daniel by the arm, firmly leading him to the rear of his house. "Come," he said.

"Where are we going?"

"Miyagi have just the thing to make you feel better."

"What? Poison?" Daniel asked, sarcastically.

Together, they walked around to Mr. Miyagi's garden. It was a beautiful and calm place where

Mr. Miyagi often meditated. Now, however, it was disordered by construction work. Mr. Miyagi, it appeared, was putting an addition on his house. The framing was up and the siding was ready to go on. The old man picked up a hammer and put it in Daniel's hand.

Daniel recalled his earliest lessons in karate. When Mr. Miyagi had wanted Daniel to learn the basic blocking techniques of karate, he had had Daniel practice the movements while doing odd jobs such as washing, painting, and sanding. At first, Daniel had resented all the work he was doing, but as he had come to understand his *sensei*'s methods, he recognized the old man's wisdom. At first, he had been angry. Now, he could joke about it. "How come every time I have problems, you have work for me to do?" Daniel asked.

"Cosmic coincidence, I guess. Now, watch," Mr. Miyagi told him. He set a nail into a piece of the siding and picked up the hammer. He drew the hammer back a foot from the nail and slammed it all the way into the wood in one deft shot. "Now you," he invited, handing Daniel the hammer.

Daniel was strong, he knew that, but he didn't know if he could hammer a long nail with one stroke. He picked up a nail and set it into the wood with a tap.

"Remember, concentrate," Mr. Miyagi reminded him. "Focus."

Daniel struck the nail with the hammer, but his blow was off-center, bending the nail with a ping and sending it clattering to the deck. It was a small failure, but it was the last straw. Daniel shook his head.

"I can't. Not today," he said, the hammer hanging dejectedly from his hand at his side.

"Why not?" Mr. Miyagi challenged him.

"I feel like my whole life is going — oh, I don't know. Like it's all out of focus." He shrugged in despair.

After taking the hammer from Daniel and dropping it to the deck, Mr. Miyagi stood in front of him, taking both of Daniel's hands and pressing them together at chest level.

"When fear losing focus, always return to basic of life."

"Praying?" Daniel asked, confused.

"Breathing. No breath, no life. Now, breathe . . . in, out."

Daniel breathed, slowly, deeply, feeling the air's healing power, sensing the calm that was coming over him. As he exhaled, Mr. Miyagi raised Daniel's hands, still clasped together, until they reached high above his head. As he inhaled again, Mr. Miyagi slowly brought them down again, returning them to the prayer position. Exhaling, Mr. Miyagi extended Daniel's hands straight out in front of him. As Daniel inhaled, he returned them to the prayer position.

"Out," he said, and Daniel reached high above himself. "In," and he returned to prayer. "Out," and he reached in front. "In," and they came back. Mr. Miyagi released Daniel's hands as he continued to follow the pattern, breathing deeply, evenly. Up, down, out, in. Daniel smiled, relaxed.

"How feel?"

"Better," Daniel nodded. "Focused."

"Good. Back to work," said Mr. Miyagi, retrieving the hammer from the ground and slapping the handle firmly into Daniel's hand. He returned to his house.

Now focused, Daniel set up a nail with a gentle tap. Then, without hesitation, he drove it straight in. With one blow. Pleased, he continued his task in earnest, his mind concentrating completely on the task, not on the night before, not on Ali. Not even on Fresno.

Several hours later, Daniel was ready for a break and when Mr. Miyagi suggested some iced tea, he readily agreed and went into the house to wash up. Before returning to the deck, Daniel went to his car to retrieve a gift he'd made for Mr. Miyagi. On his way back through the house, he stopped at Mr. Miyagi's box of war ribbons and medals, earned in the Second World War. Daniel still found it hard to believe that he actually *knew* someone who had won a Congressional Medal of Honor. He didn't understand why it seemed to mean so little to Mr. Miyagi, but he thought the present he had made would be a cure for that.

Daniel had been working in shop on a frame for the medals. He was very pleased with the way the frame had come out and now he slipped off the glass and carefully placed the Congressional medal on the black velvet, surrounding it with colorful battle ribbons. Satisfied, he smoothed the velvet and slid the glass back over the medals, snapping it into place in the frame.

"Daniel-*san?*" Mr. Miyagi called from the deck.

"Be right there," Daniel answered, quickly tightening the clasps that held the glass.

"How you feel?" Mr. Miyagi called to him, pouring iced tea.

"Better," Daniel answered, adjusting the eye hooks on the frame, hoping Mr. Miyagi would stay outside until he'd finished completely. "What am I building out there, anyway?"

"Guest room," came the answer.

Daniel slipped the picture wire through the loops. "You expecting company?" he asked.

"Expecting refugee. Come get tea, now."

"Refugee? From where?" Daniel made the last twist in the wire and stood up to go out to the deck.

"Fresno," Mr. Miyagi told him.

Daniel couldn't believe it. Had he heard that right? Quickly, he stepped out onto the deck, surprised and excited.

"Miyagi talked to mother last night, too," Mr. Miyagi explained.

"She said I could stay here?"

Mr. Miyagi nodded. Daniel beamed. "This is *great*. I can't believe it. Mr. Miyagi, you saved my life again," he said. "Thanks."

"Welcome," Mr. Miyagi told him.

Daniel had almost forgotten the frame, but his gratitude at being saved from Fresno brought him back quickly. "Here," he said, offering it carefully to his friend. "I did it in shop. It's rosewood. I thought it would be nice to show off the medal and the ribbons."

"Why?" Mr. Miyagi asked, genuinely puzzled.

Daniel was confused and a little hurt by Mr. Miyagi's response. He'd expected him to be pleased. Daniel stuttered a little.

"Well, it, I mean. . . . It says something about you . . . winning the Medal of Honor."

"What do you think it says?"

"That you're brave," Daniel answered.

"No, Daniel-*san*. Only this" — he tapped his heart — "says you're brave."

"Then what does this say you are?" Daniel asked, tapping the glass over the medal.

"Lucky."

Mr. Miyagi picked up a board, a hammer, and a nail and began to work on the guest room. But Daniel was still curious.

"What did you do to win it?"

"Not important anymore." Mr. Miyagi shrugged.

"Could you have been killed?"

"*Hai*," Mr. Miyagi nodded, answering in Japanese.

"Were you afraid?"

"Knees didn't stop shaking for a whole week after," he answered truthfully as he continued with his hammering.

"Did you kill a lot of people?"

"Unfortunately," Mr. Miyagi nodded.

"Why unfortunately? They were the enemy, weren't they?"

Mr. Miyagi laid his hammer down and turned to Daniel. He spoke calmly but firmly. "They were also people," he said.

Then Daniel began to understand. War was real. Real people fought; real people died. No wonder Mr. Miyagi didn't want to look at his medal every day. He didn't want to remember . . . every day.

Chapter 2

"Say, Mr. Miyagi? You back there?"

It was a little later the same afternoon. A man's voice came from the side of the house and was followed by the sound of the gate opening. "I knocked, but there was no answer at the door and this letter is special delivery."

The postman came into the yard to find Daniel and Mr. Miyagi hard at work on the roof of the guest room, nailing shingles to the frame. Mr. Miyagi climbed down the ladder, surprised by the intrusion.

"Yes?" he said.

"Special delivery," the man said, examining the envelope, "all the way from Okinawa."

Daniel watched as Mr. Miyagi froze, a black cloud of worry descending over his normally calm face. The postman didn't notice the change and chattered on.

"Okinawa, yeah, my brother-in-law was there when he was in the Navy. Loved it. Sign here, right on this line. . . . Thanks. You from Okinawa? Must have been hard to leave there. Don't guess you get back there much, do you?"

Mr. Miyagi did not seem to hear the man. Taking the envelope and opening it, he walked to the bench in his rock garden and began reading the letter. The postman looked at Daniel, shrugged, and left.

Slowly, Daniel descended from the roof, watching Mr. Miyagi. When he'd finished the letter, he stared off into the distance, his shoulders sagging, his eyes peering into a long ago past, a past almost forgotten. Softly, Daniel spoke to his friend.

"Mr. Miyagi?" The old man did not seem to hear. "Mr. Miyagi, is it bad news?" His eyes flicked toward Daniel.

"My father is very sick."

"I didn't know he was still alive," Daniel said, stunned, and then embarrassed, for it seemed a rude thing to say, but Mr. Miyagi was beyond reaction.

"Neither did I," he answered. Then, as if in a trance, he walked into the house, leaving Daniel alone to wonder about the mystery of his friend's past.

The next day, Daniel accompanied his friend to the passport office. Mr. Miyagi would be going to Okinawa; Daniel was going to Fresno after all. Mr. Miyagi glanced around to find his way in the room crowded with summer travelers.

"Ah, this way, Daniel," he said, pointing to the sign that said ONE-DAY SERVICE.

"I didn't know you could get a passport in a day."

"If you have next day plane ticket," he said, showing Daniel the ticket he held in his hand, along with his citizenship documents. They stood together on the short line.

"How old were you when you left Okinawa?" Daniel asked.

"Same age as you, sixteen."

"Why did you leave?"

"I fell in love with a girl," he explained.

"So?"

"It was arranged by her parents for her to marry someone else." Daniel knew that Mr. Miyagi had been married, but it was to a woman he'd met after he'd come to America, so he must have left this woman he'd loved in Okinawa. It was hard to imagine a world in which a marriage arranged by parents would be more important than the love between two people. It seemed so old-fashioned. But, looking at Mr. Miyagi's face, Daniel knew that, old-fashioned or not, it was real.

"You knew the guy she was going to marry?" he asked, curious.

"*Hai.* He was my best friend."

"Next," said the clerk. Mr. Miyagi stepped up to the counter.

That afternoon Daniel tried to learn a little more about what had happened in Okinawa as he helped Mr. Miyagi pack for the trip. He sensed that Mr. Miyagi's sadness and concern were not all because of his father's illness, and Daniel hated to see Mr. Miyagi suffer. It was as if the world was not in focus for the old man. Daniel needed to understand before he could help.

He stood staring at two photographs Mr. Miyagi had given him. One was of a beautiful Okinawan girl in formal traditional dress.

"What's her name?"

"Yukie." He pronounced it Yuki-eh.

"Is she the lady who wrote the letter? The same one you were in love with?"

"*Hai.*"

"She's beautiful," Daniel said truthfully.

"Very beautiful," Mr. Miyagi agreed.

Daniel looked at the second picture. It showed a young man in a karate gi — the traditional karate outfit — posed in a cat stance, looking lethal. His stony face showed no warmth, no compassion, no friendship. It was hard to imagine this man a friend to Mr. Miyagi.

"And this was your friend?"

"Sato." Mr. Miyagi supplied the name.

"What did he do when he found out how you felt about Yukie?"

"Challenge Miyagi to a fight."

"Why?" Such a fight sounded odd, almost primitive, to Daniel.

"To save his honor."

"And you lost?" Daniel asked, surprised. But then he looked again at the cold eyes that stared at him from the photograph.

"Didn't fight. Left Okinawa forever the next day."

"But you *loved* her —" Daniel protested.

"Very much."

"And she loved you?"

"*Hai.*"

"So how could you leave?"

"Miyagi not believe in fighting," he answered simply.

"But you two were in love."

"Never put passion before principle, Daniel-*san*. Even if you win, you lose."

Mr. Miyagi had a way of boiling complicated issues down to their simplest elements.

"You think they got married?" Daniel asked.

"His family was richest in village. Hers was poorest. It was a good arrangement."

"Then he won't be angry about his honor anymore. It was forty-five years ago," Daniel said, putting the pictures down on the table.

"In Okinawa, honor has no time limit."

"You've got to be kidding," Daniel said, amazed.

"Not kidding. See my white shirt?"

"Uh, sure," Daniel answered, startled by the return to the present. "I put it in your suitcase."

"Thank you."

"You think Sato's still alive?"

"We are the same age," Mr. Miyagi told him. Again, Daniel had trouble comprehending that the picture was of a man now past sixty, still alive, and still, even in silence, menacing Mr. Miyagi.

"I guess I'd better go home and pack my stuff for Fresno. I'll come say good-bye tomorrow."

"I'll be here. Good-night, Daniel-*san*. I'm sorry things didn't work out."

"Me, too," Daniel agreed, leaving quickly. On the front stoop, he paused to look back at his friend. Once again, Mr. Miyagi had withdrawn into his own world, a world of the past, for he sat by his open suitcase, staring at the photographs of the two people he had once cared about the most.

Daniel went home.

Chapter 3

Daniel didn't have a minute to spare. He scurried through the milling crowds in the airport, lugging the suitcase at his side. For a moment, he thought he caught a glimpse of Mr. Miyagi, but he wasn't certain. He hadn't called and he knew Mr. Miyagi would be disappointed that he hadn't visited this morning to say good-bye. Daniel hoped, though, that Mr. Miyagi would agree to his new plan. It had taken a lot of convincing, but his mother had finally agreed. She understood that a real friend wasn't someone who just said good-bye when things got difficult. Mr. Miyagi had been with Daniel when he needed help. Daniel could return the favor now.

"Gate 29-A," Daniel said to himself. "How far out can it be?" Glancing at a clock, he pushed himself to the limit.

Then Daniel saw Mr. Miyagi, just going through the door to the accordion-fold jetway that led to the waiting plane. Mr. Miyagi was the last one in line. The man's shoulders were slumped. He looked tired and lonely.

"Mr. Miyagi!" Daniel called to him. The old man turned around, surprised.

"Daniel-*san*, what are you doing here?"

Cheerfully, Daniel waved his ticket at Mr. Miyagi, knowing that Mr. Miyagi might well refuse to let him come along, but hoping that he would agree.

"I'm coming with you. My mother said it was okay and I already have a passport," Daniel explained as he neared Mr. Miyagi at the jetway door.

Mr. Miyagi raised his eyebrows and looked at Daniel. "Expensive ticket," he accused.

"I have money," Daniel protested.

"Yes. For college."

"So, I'll get a part-time job when I get back, and go to school six months later." Mr. Miyagi looked unconvinced. Daniel tried to persuade him. "Mr. Miyagi, you're more important than starting college on time. A lot more important. When I need you, you're there. I couldn't let you go alone. I mean, if it's okay with you. Besides," Daniel concluded, "it'll give me a chance to study my Okinawan history up close."

"Didn't know you studied it."

Daniel pulled a book from the pocket of his carry-on bag. "Just started," he said proudly, displaying *A Short History of Okinawa*.

Mr. Miyagi looked amused at Daniel's enthusiasm, but he remained, undecided, on the threshold of the jetway.

"We're closing the doors," the gate attendant interrupted. "You'll have to go back to the waiting area, young man," she told Daniel, having seen him, but not his ticket.

Mr. Miyagi, as usual, came to his rescue.

"Young man is coming with us," he said, as Daniel showed the woman his ticket.

Daniel's face lit up. "Thank you, Mr. Miyagi," he said, sighing with relief.

"No, Daniel-*san*. Thank *you*," his friend replied, bowing to Daniel. The attendant closed the door behind them.

Later, while the flight attendant handed out blankets and pillows, Daniel pored over the map of Okinawa that folded out of the history book.

"What did you say the name of your village is?"

"Tome," said Mr. Miyagi, pronouncing it Toe-me.

"I thought so, but I can't find it," Daniel said, shifting the map under the minispotlight above his seat, examining the island's coastline for the fishing village where Mr. Miyagi had been born.

"You find Naha?" Mr. Miyagi asked.

"Naha, yeah, here it is."

"Tome directly north, on the sea."

Daniel moved his finger up on the map, but without luck. "Only thing I see there is a big air base. Kadena. Yeah, that's all there is. No Tome. Must be really small, huh?"

"Not so small," Mr. Miyagi told him. "You find it. Look again tomorrow. Now, get some sleep."

Daniel was really too excited to sleep. It seemed

impossible. that two days ago, he had been expecting to spend the summer in Fresno. Now, here he was, flying across the Pacific Ocean to begin his summer in Okinawa. Life was full of surprises. He hoped he could help make the trip a nice surprise for Mr. Miyagi. That thought made him recall the fierce-looking man in the old photograph.

"Mr. Miyagi?"

"*Hai?*" came the muffled reply from under the blanket.

"Was Sato as good as you in karate?"

"Had same teacher."

"Your father?" Daniel asked, surprised.

"*Hai.*"

"But I thought you told me your family's karate was only taught by father to son."

"I convinced my father to make an exception in Sato's case. He was my best friend. Like brother. Now, good-night, Daniel-*san.*"

Daniel pulled the blanket up to his neck and tried to scrunch the little pillow under his head so he could get some sleep, but his mind was racing.

"Mr. Miyagi?"

"Hmmm?" was the sleepy answer.

"If you had fought Sato, would your father have been the referee?"

"Would have been no referee."

"So, how do you tell who wins?"

"Whoever's dead doesn't." With that, Mr. Miyagi pulled the blanket up over his head and was soon asleep.

Daniel, on the other hand, was wide awake.

As it had never occurred to him that enemies who died in wars were real people, it had also never occurred to him that karate matches could end in the death of one of the opponents. In a real way, he had known that Mr. Miyagi *could* have killed Kreese in the parking lot, but he hadn't. He wouldn't. Daniel understood, though, that Mr. Miyagi would have had to kill Sato. Once more, the memory of that angrily determined face in the photo came to him and kept him wide awake long into the night over the Pacific.

Chapter 4

Once through customs, Daniel and Mr. Miyagi entered the passenger terminal at Naha Field in Okinawa. It seemed to Daniel a very odd combination of ancient Orient and New World — of Japan and the U.S.A. From his history book, Daniel had learned that the U.S. had occupied Okinawa from the end of the Second World War until 1972, at which time it had turned the governing of the island over to Japan. Okinawa was still home for several major U.S. military bases.

Everywhere, signs and advertisements beckoned customers in both English and Japanese. U.S. servicemen and their families mingled comfortably with the local population. Following Mr. Miyagi to the airport exit, Daniel could not keep his eyes off the sights. Suddenly, a familiar face stared at him from one of the advertising posters on the walls.

"Hey, Mr. Miyagi, look!" Daniel called, halting his friend and pointing to the ad. From high above them on the poster the menacing features of a much older Sato glared in icy fury while his right hand smashed through twelve one-inch wooden boards, the splinters of wood exploding outward from the blow. Beneath the photograph were the words:

LEARN KARATE FROM MASTER SATO
AT OKINAWA'S BIGGEST DOJO
FORTY YEARS OFFICIAL INSTRUCTOR
TO THE U.S. MILITARY
PROVEN IN COMBAT.

"Isn't that him?" Daniel asked in awe.

"*Hai*," he answered, frowning.

"Can *you* break wood like that?"

Mr. Miyagi sniffed in disdain. "Don't know," he answered. "Never been attacked by tree." He continued to press toward the door where they could get a taxi, and Daniel followed him.

As they reached the exit, however, Daniel suddenly saw a young man wearing dark glasses. He seemed to be about Daniel's age and was carrying a walkie-talkie in one hand and a sign in the other that read MIYAGI.

"Gee, is that guy here to pick *us* up?"

Mr. Miyagi seemed surprised, but approached the man with the sign.

"Miyagi-*san?*" the young man asked, reverently. When Mr. Miyagi nodded, the man bowed. "It is a great honor," he told them and guided them to an old Cadillac limousine. While their luggage was stored in the trunk by the driver, the young man held the rear door of the car open for them.

"Yukie-*san* could not meet you herself to escort you home," the man said, in explanation. "I am Chozen Toguchi."

"I'm Daniel LaRusso," Daniel told him, gratefully climbing into the limousine.

"How did anyone know I was coming?" Mr. Miyagi asked suspiciously.

"Okinawa is a very small place," Chozen explained. Warily, Mr. Miyagi joined Daniel in the car. The door closed and they pulled away from the curb.

Daniel was almost too busy taking in his first real look at Okinawa to notice that Mr. Miyagi was very uneasy. The old man sat erect and stared intently through the glass partition that separated them from Chozen and the driver, oblivious to the muted strains of heavy metal rock that blasted from the car's radio, but keenly alert to impending danger. Daniel's sight-seeing was interrupted by Mr. Miyagi's vigorous tapping on the partition. The driver slid the glass open and leaned his head back to hear Mr. Miyagi over the blare of the radio.

"Isn't the village that way?" he asked, indicating a road to the left.

"Some things have changed since you left, Miyagi-*san*," the driver offered in answer.

"And some things have not," Chozen added, ominously. The glass partition slid shut and the car drove on.

Suddenly the car made a sharp turn toward a large airplane hangar. The hangar doors opened and the limo slid into the darkened building, drawing to a stop in the single circle of light. The hangar doors shut behind them. The driver and

Chozen quickly got out of the car and pulled open the doors for Daniel and Mr. Miyagi.

"Out!" Chozen commanded. His thin layer of politeness was gone. Perplexed, Daniel and Mr. Miyagi obeyed, and then watched as a third young man appeared from the darkness. He opened the trunk and removed their luggage.

"What *is* this?" Daniel asked angrily.

"Quiet!" was all the answer Chozen gave Daniel as he faced into the dark shadows of the cavernous hangar. "Uncle," he called, his voice echoing through the building. A few seconds later, measured footsteps responded from the darkness. Frozen in fear, Daniel watched as the outline of a figure emerged, striding imperiously, halting at the edge of the light.

"Sato-*san*," Mr. Miyagi said.

"So, coward, you have returned," Sato accused.

"To settle affairs with my father."

"And with me," he pronounced.

Mr. Miyagi sighed in resignation. "I will not fight."

"Then you will die as you have lived. A coward. See your father. Then you see me." The finality of the words echoed in the empty hangar.

With that, Chozen opened the rear door of the car for Sato, who disappeared behind the mask of its darkened windows. Chozen began to shut the door, then paused, reaching down into the car and emerging with Daniel's book about Okinawa in his hand. He gave Daniel a look of disgust and threw the book at his feet in challenge. Chozen closed Sato's door and then joined his companions in the front seat. Dramatically, the limousine squealed out through the rear door of the hangar, leaving Daniel and Mr. Miyagi and their luggage stranded in the island of light.

"Come, Daniel-*san*," Mr. Miyagi told him, reaching for his suitcase. "We get taxi now."

Chapter 5

The uneven ride became bumpy; the bumpy ride
became jarring. The taxi met the next pothole
with bone-rattling impact and then slid to a stop
in the mud next to a construction site. Daniel and
Mr. Miyagi waited in the backseat of the cab
while a young American soldier navigated around
the trench where jackhammers tore at the old
roadway, and leaned into the taxi window.

"Where you going, buddy?"

The cabdriver began talking in a confusion of
Japanese, apparently speaking no English. Mr.
Miyagi answered for him.

"Tome village," he told the soldier.

The soldier frowned and shook his head, be-
wildered. "Never heard of it. This is Kadena Air
Base. Hey, Sarge . . ." he called to another soldier. "Ever hear of Tome village?"

"We're standing on it," explained the sergeant.
"Take that road," he said, pointing to the right.

The driver put the car into reverse and backed
out of the construction site, rocking his passen-
gers as he maneuvered among the potholes once

again. Finally, he swung the vehicle onto the road the sergeant had indicated. It led down the side of the mountain in a series of S-curves, to the village of Tome — or what was left of it after the building of Kadena Air Base. Mr. Miyagi was silent for the remainder of the trip. Daniel thought he was probably trying to see the village as he had known it forty-five years earlier, so he left his friend to his recollections.

What Daniel saw was another example of the joining of old and new in Okinawa. Tome was a small village on the edge of the sea. The houses were crowded together on the hillside. The buildings were small with no apparent signs of prosperity — few cars, few tv antennas, no swimming pools or even pleasure boats in the beautiful natural harbor below.

The people who walked down the spotlessly clean streets stared at the taxi. Daniel and Mr. Miyagi stared back. Some of them wore traditional Japanese clothes. Others wore more familiar blue jeans and sweat shirts, or GI garb that must have come from the air base. A small shop displayed Japanese groceries in the window, but over the door was a too-familiar sign that said, in English, "Drink Coca-Cola." The movie theater down the street advertised in Japanese, but the picture in the display case by the door was of Sylvester Stallone in boxer shorts.

Soon, the taxi drew up to the curb and stopped. They were before a one-story building. The house was set back from the street and had a small but exquisitely tended garden in front of it, welcoming visitors. A wooden fence to the side surrounded what Daniel presumed was the more formal garden within the house.

Daniel removed the luggage from the trunk while Mr. Miyagi paid for the taxi. Then, as Daniel watched, Mr. Miyagi approached the door uncertainly, obviously both anxious and excited. He reached for the doorknob and hesitated. Then, instead, he knocked on the door of his old home, as if he were a stranger.

Almost immediately, the door was opened. Daniel could hardly believe what he saw, for he could have sworn it was the sixteen-year-old girl in the picture Mr. Miyagi had shown him of Yukie. But she would be almost sixty years old now! Whoever it was, she was beautiful and Daniel was stunned.

"Miyagi-*san*," the girl said, excitedly. "Auntie Yukie said you would come —"

"Where is she?" he asked.

"Nursing your father," the young woman answered, indicating a room behind her. Quickly, Mr. Miyagi entered the house and went to the rear. Daniel followed him, carrying their luggage. As he passed the girl their eyes met and she smiled at him. She was even more beautiful when she smiled.

"My name's Daniel," he told her.

"I am Kumiko," she said, and then rushed ahead to open the door for Mr. Miyagi so he could see his father.

There in the room, Daniel saw an older woman with gray hair. He recognized her as the Yukie of Mr. Miyagi's picture, for the beauty of her youth was still visible forty-five years later. At first she was unaware of their presence, caught up in tending to the old man who lay on a Japanese bed, breathing unevenly.

"Auntie Yukie," Kumiko spoke quietly. The woman looked up, caught by surprise to see Mr. Miyagi. Her face revealed nothing, but her body shivered involuntarily in recognition.

Silently, Mr. Miyagi entered the room and knelt by his father, opposite Yukie. He looked at the old man's face, examining it, almost as he had been examining the village — looking for the familiar, looking through nearly half a century past.

"He is asleep," Yukie told him. Mr. Miyagi nodded and continued his watch. Finally, he looked up at Yukie.

"How did you know where to find me?" he asked.

"Have known for years," she told him.

"Then why did you not write sooner?"

"Out of respect."

"For your husband?" he asked.

"No, for your silence," she said. "I never married."

At that moment, Mr. Miyagi's father stirred. His eyes flickered open and he looked up in confusion. He closed and then opened his eyes once more, straining to focus. He, too, seemed to be looking through a mist of forty-five years. Tears of joy filled his eyes and he reached weakly to touch Mr. Miyagi's face. As he caressed his son, he spoke to him in Japanese.

Daniel looked to Kumiko for an explanation, noticing that her eyes glistened with emotion.

"What did he say?" he asked.

She translated for him, deeply moved: " 'If I

am dreaming, let me never awake. If I am awake, let me never sleep.' "

Mr. Miyagi held his father's hands in his own and they spoke to each other in silence.

Gracefully, Yukie gathered up the bedside tray and left the room, bowing to Daniel. Kumiko followed her, pausing to look at Daniel once more and to smile at him as she had before. Daniel was really starting to like that smile.

Chapter 6

Daniel sat up in bed and rubbed his eyes in sleepy confusion. With a start, he realized that he was in the Okinawan village of Tome, six thousand miles, one day, and a whole civilization away from home. No wonder he was confused.

Quickly, he grabbed his clothes and slipped into them, eager to see what today would bring, hoping he could be of some help to Mr. Miyagi. His friend certainly needed it.

There hadn't been time to see the whole house the night before, so Daniel proceeded cautiously through the sliding paper doors called *shoji*. He slid one aside to reveal the formal garden. In one half of it, the plants, trees, bonsai, rocks, and water all combined to make this space beautiful and serene. It was spotlessly clean and perfectly trimmed. This was a garden for the spirit.

The other half of the garden was for the body, for it was a working farmer's garden, meticulously tended and planted with radishes. Green leaves stood guard over the crop beneath the soil. In spite of the marked difference between the two parts of the garden, it was a great place to be, as if all material and spiritual needs could be met on one piece of earth.

Looking at the family garden made Daniel think of Mr. Miyagi. Hesitantly, he called for him. "Mr. Miyagi?" There was no answer.

Daniel's eye was caught by a slightly open *shoji* door in another building on the property. He walked over and opened it. For the second time that morning, he was surprised by what he saw, for this was the Miyagi family *dojo* — their karate gym. Daniel removed his shoes, entered, and looked around, soaking in the sight.

It was a single room, perhaps thirty feet square. The floor was covered by an enormous *tatami* mat, woven of rice straw, meant to soften the fall of combatants who might unwillingly land on it. The walls of the *dojo* were lined with photographs and paintings. Daniel realized that these pictures must be of four hundred years of karate-practicing Miyagis, and he found it humbling to be in this shrine to karate. Above all the others was a painting of one man in formal garb that appeared to be very ancient, though, as Daniel knew, traditions lived long on this island. The man's round face and small mouth looked so much like Mr. Miyagi that Daniel almost had to laugh at the thought of his friend got up in the antique outfit.

Daniel's attention was next drawn to a hanging sack of rice near one wall. He recognized that this must be a tool of learning, much like the boxer's punching bag. He pummeled the rice bag hesitantly, and was immediately sorry because it was very heavy and very hard. Rubbing his hand, he turned again, this time to examine the display of Okinawan weapons shelved on the far wall of the *dojo*. He'd never seen anything like this collection except in a museum, for there were several long sticks, knotted ropes, spears, and cloth body protectors.

Then at the end of the case was a strange drum-like object that certainly didn't seem to belong with a collection of weapons. It had a round frame, perhaps four inches in diameter, over which was stretched the drumskin. A straight handle extended from the frame, in lollipop fashion. Attached to the frame, at the sides, two wooden balls hung from short thongs like limp arms. As Daniel picked it up by the handle the balls began banging against the skin. Startled by the noise, he silenced the drum, holding the wooden balls.

"So, how you like Miyagi family *dojo*?" Mr. Miyagi asked, standing at the door.

"It's great," Daniel answered with enthusiasm. "Who are all these people?" He indicated the pictures on the wall.

"Miyagis. Four hundred years' worth."

"Who is he?" Daniel asked, pointing to the largest painting, the one of the man who looked like Mr. Miyagi.

"Miyagi Shimpo Sensei," the old man told him, bowing respectfully at the picture. "First Miyagi to bring karate to Okinawa."

"He's the one who went to China?" Daniel asked, remembering that Mr. Miyagi had once told him that his family had brought the art from China to Okinawa.

"Hai. In 1625."

Daniel was struck by the enormity of such a trip three hundred and sixty years ago. "How did he get there? By boat?"

"By accident," Mr. Miyagi answered, then added, "Like all Miyagi, he was a fisherman. Shimpo Sensei love fishing. Loved *sake* — Japanese wine. One day, strong *sake*, strong sun, strong wind, no fish. Shimpo Sensei fell asleep off coast of Okinawa. Woke off coast of China. Ten years later, he comes back with Chinese wife, two kids." He paused. "And secret of Miyagi family karate." He tapped the drum in Daniel's hand.

"This is the secret of your karate?" Daniel asked skeptically, looking at the drum once more.

"Hai." Mr. Miyagi took the drum from Daniel and began to twirl it deftly. As soon as the motion began, the wooden balls came to life, whacking at the drumskin, producing a loud rat-tat-tat-tatting. It was quite unlike the tentative thumping Daniel had been able to produce from the drum. It was a pleasing sound in its own noisy way, but it certainly didn't look like karate to Daniel.

"I don't get it."

Mr. Miyagi handed the drum to him, nodding with certainty. "Practice. You will understand. Come. Time for work."

Together they left the *dojo* and walked out through the garden to the street, passing the doorway where Yukie tended to Mr. Miyagi's father.

Daniel looked with wonder at the town, which stood on a hillside leading down to the sea. They could hear traditional Japanese music wafting on the air. Daniel could almost believe he'd traveled back nearly four hundred years to Miyagi Shimpo Sensei's time in Tome. Daniel could picture him in his mind's eye setting out one fine morning in his fishing boat. But then Daniel realized there were no fishing boats in the little harbor at the foot of the hill.

"Where are all the fishing boats?" he asked. "Out at sea already?"

"Sold."

"Sold? How do you know that?"

"Yukie told me. After the war, someone brought in big commercial fishing boats. In two years, fish were all gone. Waters fished out."

"Who did it?" Daniel asked him.

"Only one who could afford it: Sato. Only thing left is old cannery." Mr. Miyagi pointed to a shabby untended building down the hill near the docks.

Together, they continued walking toward the cannery. On the steps of the village shrine, there was an old man dressed in a strange outfit. Daniel realized this must be a monk. He was strumming a stringed instrument, the source of the traditional music they'd heard, teaching a few of the boys in the village how to play. He waved warmly to Mr. Miyagi and Mr. Miyagi returned the greeting.

"The day I left, he was in the same place, doing the same thing," he told Daniel.

Daniel smiled in response and then returned to the earlier subject. "Must have been tough times with the fish gone."

"Many people moved to the city for work. Father and others invented a new economy," he said, pointing to the gardens and vegetables being boxed for market at one of the buildings. "Saved what was left of the village," he said with pride.

"So everyone owns his own little business —"

"Sato owns," Mr. Miyagi corrected him. "Village rents." Daniel realized that Sato's grip was not only on Mr. Miyagi, but on the whole village, for he held their livelihood in his hands.

The two friends walked in front of a school and saw that Kumiko was teaching a group of young girls to dance. She smiled at Daniel and he waved to her. The girls began giggling at their teacher and whispering among themselves. In mock severity, Kumiko called them to attention as Daniel and Mr. Miyagi continued down the road.

"They practice for *O-bon* festival."

"In honor of the dead," Daniel supplied.

"Very good," said Mr. Miyagi, impressed.

"I read about it. Look at that — a pill box probably left over from the war," Daniel said, pointing to a large metal door leading to a fortified gun emplacement — a World War II bunker.

"Must be. Crazy Yamaguchi's house used to be there."

"What do you think they use it for?" Daniel asked.

In answer, Mr. Miyagi called to a nearby villager and spoke with him in Japanese.

"Storm shelter," Mr. Miyagi explained and they continued on their walk.

As they came to a crossroad, however, they

were suddenly brought up short, for Sato's large limousine screeched to a halt before them, blocking their way. Two of the young men they'd seen in the hangar emerged from the front doors of the car and, in military unison, opened the rear doors from which Chozen and Sato stepped. As the three young men stood in stony silence, Sato confronted Daniel and Mr. Miyagi.

"You have seen your father," Sato pronounced. It was an accusation.

"Yes."

"Then we finish tonight. I will bring my nephew as witness."

"Two of you will lose a night's sleep. I will not come."

From behind Sato, Chozen shouted at Mr. Miyagi, "You are a stinking coward!" Sato turned and silenced his nephew with a stare. He then returned to glare at Mr. Miyagi.

"You leave me no choice," he said, bowing to Mr. Miyagi. Mr. Miyagi stood motionless, arms at his sides. Two feet away, Sato settled into a karate stance, knees flexed. Slowly and deliberately, he sited on Mr. Miyagi with one hand on Mr. Miyagi's heart while he drew the other back into a fist — the same fist that could break twelve inches of wood, but this time the target was Mr. Miyagi's heart.

Daniel was frozen in fear; Chozen's eyes glistened with excitement; Mr. Miyagi stood calmly; Sato's features were cold with concentration. His fist was coiled and ready to strike.

"Miyagi-*san*! Miyagi-*san*!" It was Yukie running down the street toward them. She stopped in surprise at the sight that greeted her and then was stunned into completing her mission.

"Your father," she said, her voice filled with sadness. "He asks for you. And," she said, turning to Sato, "you."

Sato quit his karate pose and nodded respectfully. Together they walked rapidly back up the hill to Mr. Miyagi's house, followed by Daniel and Yukie.

In the darkened room, Daniel watched as Mr. Miyagi knelt on one side of his father, Sato on the other. The old man, whose breathing was shallow and pained, opened his eyes to Mr. Miyagi and Sato. His frail left hand took one of Sato's hands, his right reached for his son's. With his remaining strength, he drew their hands together until they touched, his hands uniting theirs over his body. The old man looked at his son and then at his student, a smile creasing his lips. With that, his eyes seemed to dim and the strength left his hands clasped above him. They all watched as the old man's life escaped.

After a moment, Mr. Miyagi looked back up at Sato, but the other man's face hardened. He withdrew his hand coldly from Mr. Miyagi's grasp, and stood up. Looking down at Mr. Miyagi, he spoke.

"Out of respect for my teacher, I allow you your period to mourn. When it is over, I will be back."

He bowed deeply to the old man's body, and

then strode out of the house, brushing gruffly past Yukie, Kumiko, and Daniel.

At the bedside, Mr. Miyagi looked at his father and lovingly stroked his head, pushing his hair off his forehead, and gently closed the old man's eyes for the last time.

Chapter 7

Mr. Miyagi bore his grief in silence, offering little opportunity for Daniel to console him, except to keep his friend company. During the funeral and the traditional mourning period, Daniel stood by him; as Mr. Miyagi sorted through his father's things, sparking bittersweet memories of his childhood, Daniel stood by him; as he stared out over the lagoon, filled with sadness and remorse, Daniel stood by him, knowing, then, it was time for some comforting words. Daniel joined Mr. Miyagi on the promontory rock by the lagoon.

"You know," Daniel began, "when my father died, I spent a lot of time thinking I wasn't such a great son. Like, maybe, I should have listened more. Or spent more time together with him. I felt so guilty, you know, like he had done everything for me. And I had done nothing for him. And then one day I realized that I had done the greatest thing for him before he died." Mr. Miyagi continued to stare at the water. Daniel continued: "I cared about him. I held his hand and said good-bye."

Still, Mr. Miyagi didn't respond. Daniel looked over at him and saw that tears streamed down his cheeks. Daniel reached around his friend's shoulder and held his arm there in comfort. He knew that if Mr. Miyagi could now cry, he could heal.

Daniel and Mr. Miyagi faced each other in the Miyagi *dojo*. While Mr. Miyagi threw punches and kicks at Daniel, Daniel blocked them. The workout felt good — to both of them. The unspoken message between them was that it was a real return to normal. Punch. Hand up to block. Kick. Arm out to block. Punch. Hand down to block. Mr. Miyagi's measured cries of *kiai!* punctuated their exercise.

"Always look," he warned Daniel, correcting his sideways block. "Focus at last minute," he said, and then bowed to Daniel. The lesson was over. Mr. Miyagi turned to the collection of pictures and began to hang up a final one — the picture of his own father — in the last available space. Daniel walked over to the weapon case and began to play with the drum.

"Mr. Miyagi, I don't understand something," he said, puzzled.

"What's that, Daniel-*san*?" he answered, adjusting the picture on the hook.

"If Sato hates you so much, why'd he give you time to mourn?"

"Because my father was his teacher. In his

45

heart, Sato-*san* still knows right from wrong."

"But he still wants to kill you."

"Sometimes, what the heart knows, the head forgets," he said in explanation.

"But he's looking to go to war."

"Don't stop war by participating in one, Daniel-*san*."

"But if he had thrown that punch at you by the car, what would you have done?"

"Blocked."

"You think you could have?" Daniel asked, dubious.

"Even *you* could."

"I'm not that strong."

"Not a matter of who's strong," Mr. Miyagi told him, tapping his bicep. "Matter of who's smarter," he said, tapping Daniel's head.

"Smarter?" Daniel didn't understand.

"Come, I will demonstrate," he said, turning to leave the *dojo*. Eager and curious, Daniel followed him.

A few minutes later, they stood by the deserted, ramshackle cannery. Above the door, there was a sign in English and Japanese that read SATO CANNERY. The ruin of what had once been the principal business in the town seemed to Daniel like an ever-present reminder of Sato's disdain for the people of Tome.

"From my first karate lesson, father always said best block is no block," Mr. Miyagi told him.

"I don't get it."

"That's what I said until I worked here. First job," he said, recalling the past. Quickly, they went through the broken door, past the abandoned rows of work tables where once much of Tome had been employed canning the catch the rest of the town brought from the sea.

They left the main room and walked to the outdoor docking area where the fish had been unloaded from the boats. A vicious-looking hook with three prongs, attached to a chain and pulley, still held rotting fishnets. Mr. Miyagi reached for the chain, put it in Daniel's hand, and then began climbing up a small ladder.

"The fish went from the boat into the net, then across here," he said, indicating where he was walking, a distance of ten yards from where the boat would have been. He then climbed a smaller ladder to a platform in front of a large wooden chute, blocked now by two wooden guardrails. "To here," he said, pointing to the chute and maintaining a delicate balance on the precarious ledge where someone must have had to stand to open the nets and release the fish into the chute.

Daniel stood by the hook, looking at its deadly prongs, undulled by the years, in spite of their coating of rust.

"One day, Miyagi's mind was somewhere else when the fish came across. Now push, Daniel," he ordered.

Daniel pulled the chain, sending the hook, nets and all, down the track toward the chute. At the last possible instant, Mr. Miyagi sidestepped, moving from the opening of the chute. With a sickening crunch, the hooks pierced the wooden guardrails as if they were paper, dumping the rotten nets onto the chute. The damage was exactly where Mr. Miyagi had stood one split second earlier.

"Now you understand?" Mr. Miyagi asked. Daniel nodded. He could easily picture that the best way to block a punch was to not be there when the punch landed.

"Yeah," he said. "Now I understand."

"Good. Come," Mr. Miyagi said, turning to go.

"Can I try first?" Daniel asked. Mr. Miyagi paused in thought and then his eyes lit on some big cork fishing floats on the floor by the dock and he nodded.

"Release the hook," Mr. Miyagi said. Quickly, Daniel climbed up by the chute and untangled the hook from the splinters and the nets and sent it careening back down the track to Mr. Miyagi, who blunted it with the cork, leaving it dangerous, but not deadly. Daniel stood, poised for action.

"When I say move, move," Mr. Miyagi instructed him. With amazing speed, the corked hook came flying at Daniel, on target with his stomach. Daniel stood frozen, waiting for the word from his teacher.

"Move!" the cry came. But Daniel wasn't fast enough. The heavy hook rammed into his stomach, doubling him over in pain.

"Okay, Daniel-*san*?"

Weakly, and with a grimace, Daniel answered him. "Yeah," he said, swinging the chain back to Mr. Miyagi. Once again, he took his position.

"Okay, I'm ready, Mr. Miyagi. Blast off!"

Mr. Miyagi hesitated, but then swung the chain to send the hook toward Daniel. At the last second, Mr. Miyagi cried, "Move!" Daniel moved, faster this time, but still, it wasn't enough. The hook hit him in the shoulder and sent him sprawling off the platform. Just before he tumbled all the way to the floor of the docking area, Daniel grabbed the edge of the platform. For a moment, he dangled in space. Then, slowly, he pulled himself up and swung the chain back to Mr. Miyagi.

"Maybe we try again tomorrow," the old man suggested. Daniel's answer was to stand tall in determination.

"Ready," he told Mr. Miyagi.

"Okay, but last one."

For the third time, the hook came swiftly toward Daniel. He did not flinch. He waited for the word. It came.

"Move!"

Smoothly, he moved to the side in time to watch the corked hook bounce harmlessly against the opening of the chute. Mr. Miyagi burst into applause, then pulled back the hook.

"Thanks," Daniel said, satisfied, and turned to climb down the ladder.

"You know, Daniel-*san*, there is a quality, very special, we call karate-smart. Only few people have it." Mr. Miyagi removed the cork from the hook as he spoke this high praise to his student. "I think you are one of those people," he said, releasing the hook.

Suddenly, there was the sound of the hook careening toward the chute. Daniel sprang back up to the platform and stood in ready stance. Just as the deadly hooks reached the edge of the platform, Daniel slipped to the side. There was a loud sound of cloth ripping the instant before the hook hit the wooden guardrail. When Daniel turned around, he held his hand across his stomach. As Mr. Miyagi watched in sick anticipation, Daniel moved his hand from his stomach to reveal a shredded gash across his ruined shirt and his unscathed stomach beneath. He smiled triumphantly and waited for his praise.

"Daniel-*san*."

"Yes?" he answered, expectantly.

"I take back what I said." Mr. Miyagi then harrumphed in exasperation and left the cannery. Daniel paused for a moment, looking at the piece of his shirt pinioned to the wood by the deadly hook. He ran his finger across his stomach. Involuntarily, he shivered.

Daniel caught up with Mr. Miyagi and they walked back toward the house together. On the way, they passed Chozen working with Taro, Sato's driver. They were overseeing the loading of a truck of vegetables. Each of the farmers brought his produce to the scale. Chozen noted the weight and made payment while the produce was put into the truck. On it, there was a sign, in English and Japanese, reading SATO PRODUCE.

When they were past the truck, Daniel spoke: "Does he own everything?"

"Almost."

From behind them, Chozen yelled at them: "Hey coward! Hey coward!" Taro joined in the taunting. Mr. Miyagi acted as if he had not heard, but Daniel turned to answer their charges. However, before he could speak, he thought better of it and checked his anger.

When he'd caught up with Mr. Miyagi, he asked, "Doesn't that bother you?"

Mr. Miyagi shrugged. "Why should it?" he asked.

"Because other people might believe it's true."

"A lie becomes truth only if you want to believe it, Daniel-*san*." He turned to go back to his house.

Something had caught Daniel's eye. "I'll be back a little later, Mr. Miyagi. See you," he said.

"Be wise, Daniel-*san*."

"You mean use my karate-smarts?" he asked.

"Hmph," was all the older man answered, leaving Daniel on the street.

Chapter 8

What Daniel had seen was the old monk, Ichiro, struggling with a wheelbarrow full of produce, apparently bound for Sato's truck. The front wheel of the barrow slid into a rut on the dirt road and, before Daniel could get there to help him, Ichiro's wheelbarrow toppled sideways, dumping his harvest of carrots onto the ground. Ichiro lost his balance, too, and sprawled helplessly next to the carrots.

"Are you okay?" Daniel asked, giving the man a hand to help him stand. Ichiro strained to stand, but didn't answer Daniel's question because, of course, he couldn't speak English. The hours Daniel had spent with the phrase book now paid off. *"Ikaga desu ka?"* he asked, speaking the Japanese for "How are you?"

Ichiro's face brightened and he nodded. *"Hai.* Okay," but when he stooped to gather his carrots, he winced in pain.

"Here, I'll do it," said Daniel in English, having run out of appropriate Japanese phrases, but he made himself clear with hand signals and began scooping up the carrots and filling the righted wheelbarrow while Ichiro stood nearby, rubbing his sore hip, and chattering cheerfully to Daniel in incomprehensible Japanese.

"There you are. Good as new," Daniel said, picking up the last carrot. *"Ninjin.* Right?" he asked, hoping he had the right word for carrot.

"Hai. Hai. Hai," Ichiro nodded. Then he tapped his own chest. "Ichiro," he said.

Daniel tapped himself. "Daniel," he said.

Ichiro repeated the name tentatively. "Dan-yehr," it came out.

Daniel nodded happily, and then hefted the handles of the wheelbarrow to take the carrots to Sato's truck. As Daniel loaded the carrots onto the old-fashioned balance scale, he heard Chozen speaking to Taro in Japanese. The wise-guy tone of voice was unmistakable, being the same in any language, and Daniel knew they were speaking about him. They both laughed. Ichiro scolded them, but they ignored him.

"I said your teacher should get a hearing aid." Chozen translated the words for the benefit of Daniel — who ignored them. "Maybe you need one, too," Chozen taunted.

"I only hear what's worth listening to," Daniel said evenly.

Chozen scowled at Daniel and then turned his attention to Taro, who called out the weight of Ichiro's carrots. Chozen was drawing the check for Ichiro, and Daniel went to take the carrots down and put them in the truck. By accident, he lost his grip. The sack of carrots knocked into the stack of weights on the other side of the scale, sending them tumbling to the ground.

"Sorry," said Daniel, embarrassed. He bent to pick up the weights, although Taro tried very hard to get there first. Daniel grabbed the largest weight in one hand, and gathered the two smaller ones in his other. Something seemed odd to him, though. Quickly, Taro grabbed the weights from him and put them back on the scale for the next farmer's vegetable weighing.

"Come on," Chozen told him sharply. "We're working here." The next farmer was ready to put his tomatoes on the scale. But suddenly Daniel understood.

"Wait a sec," he said, and the farmer put his tomatoes on the ground. Daniel reached for the two small weights and pointed at the larger weight. *"Onaji?"* he asked Ichiro. (Same?)

"Hai. Onaji mono desu." (Yes. They are the same.)

Daniel took the weights to the scale, putting the larger on one side, the two small ones, supposedly equal to the larger, on the other. Chozen watched him in stony silence. It didn't take long. As soon as the second small weight was placed on the balance, the scale thudded out of balance. The two smaller weights were heavier than the large weight. The weights had been tampered with; the villagers had been cheated and they knew it. Chozen was besieged by villagers scrambling to pull their own produce out of the truck and demanding that it be reweighed. In disgust, he apologized to each one, trying to pacify them all, but it was doing him little good and the vicious look he gave Daniel told him that, as far as Chozen was concerned, this episode was not finished.

Satisfied that he had done his best for justice, Daniel left Chozen to the mercy of the unhappy villagers.

Chapter 9

"Come, Daniel-*san*, time for dinner," Mr. Miyagi told him, leading him through the *shoji* to the dining room. When Daniel stepped through the door, he stopped and stared, for the table, barely ten inches above the floor and set for two, was laid with the most incredible array of dishes he'd ever seen. Yukie and Kumiko, dressed in traditional kimonos, were kneeling to the side of the table, near the other door in the room that must have led to the kitchen.

Daniel tugged at Mr. Miyagi's sleeve. "It's only set for two," he whispered.

"Very observant," Mr. Miyagi responded, entering the room and sitting cross-legged on the floor at the table. Ceremoniously, he bowed to Yukie and Kumiko. They bowed to him in acknowledgment. Daniel followed Mr. Miyagi's lead and took the other seat at the table, bowing to the women, who bowed back to him.

As soon as they were seated comfortably, Yukie came forward and knelt next to Mr. Miyagi. Gracefully, she picked up one of the dishes on the table and held it for Mr. Miyagi. He picked up his chopsticks and selected a morsel from the plate. He tasted it and nodded politely in satisfaction. Yukie smiled slightly and put the dish in front of him. It reminded Daniel of nothing so much as the ceremony he'd watched in restaurants to open a bottle of wine. Briefly, he wondered what would have happened if Mr. Miyagi hadn't liked the taste he'd had, but he decided that Mr. Miyagi would never have been so rude as that.

Daniel was brought back from his musings by the realization that Kumiko was now kneeling next to him and holding a dish for his approval. He took the chopsticks in his hand, very carefully grasped a bite of food for himself, and tasted it in the same tentative manner Mr. Miyagi had assumed. The morsel tasted a little strange, but it was okay. It was cold and had a slight tangy flavor accompanying the seafood taste. There was an unusual sort of crunch to it, too. He'd never tasted anything quite like it.

"Hey, that's good," he said approvingly, skipping the polite nod he'd seen Mr. Miyagi give. "It's kind of like a Japanese Caesar salad. What's in it?" As soon as he'd asked the question, he was afraid it was a mistake. He was right.

"Pickled octopus feet, raw sea urchin, and seaweed," Kumiko told him proudly. He stopped chewing.

"Kumiko dove off reef for the urchins herself," Mr. Miyagi told him. Daniel began chewing. Very carefully.

"You like?" Kumiko asked expectantly.

He swallowed.

"Yeah. It's great," Daniel told her, hoping the smile on his face looked more sincere than it felt. She smiled back at him, beaming with pride. With determination born of good manners, he took another mouthful and cast his eyes over the table again, wondering what the *other* dishes had in them. Mr. Miyagi didn't seem to notice Daniel's dilemma, so Daniel decided to ignore it, too. It helped when he thought about what Kumiko's reaction might be to two all beef patties, special sauce, lettuce, cheese, pickles, onions. . . .

After dinner, Kumiko disappeared into the kitchen and Mr. Miyagi and Yukie walked toward the lagoon together. Daniel thought they must have many things to discuss and so left them alone. On his own, he fetched the hand drum from the *dojo* and took it into the garden, where he tried to understand its secret. He twirled it, producing the rat-tat-tatting Mr. Miyagi had showed him. The more he watched it, the more it looked to him like arms blocking and then striking out at an opponent. He set the drum down on a bench and tried to swing his arms like the wooden balls of the drum. He was not satisfied with the results. The effort reminded him of the time he had tried to teach himself karate out of a book. And it was equally unsuccessful this time. Still he persisted, improving the movement slightly with each attempt. He found it worked best if he pivoted on his left foot, swinging the right out for counterweight and momentum, letting centrifugal force lift his arms as it did the balls on the drum. But as a karate move it seemed to him more graceful than deadly; and on him, Daniel freely admitted, it wasn't even graceful. He tried it again. Same result. He tried once more.

As he swung around, he found himself face to face with Kumiko, now wearing modern clothes: a pair of faded jeans, a turtleneck, and a sweat shirt decorated with splashes of color. In any language, she was beautiful.

"Hello," she said.

"Hi." Daniel regained his balance, hoping he hadn't looked too ridiculous.

"I'm disturbing you?"

"No. Not at all. I was just, uh. . . . Hey, thanks for dinner," he said, changing the subject. "It was great."

"You really liked it?"

"Yeah, I did."

"We were afraid it would be too — uh, what is the word? — too . . . exotic."

"That's my middle name," Daniel assured her.

"Excuse, please?" Kumiko looked at him confused.

"It means you like something a lot, understand?"

"*Hai.*" She nodded, and then looked at the drum, which was on the bench. "What were you doing?" she asked.

"Practicing some moves."

"Moves? What are moves?"

"You know, like karate?"

"Looks like Bon dance, not karate," she told him, confirming his worst suspicions.

"Yeah, well, I must be doing something wrong."

"No. Doing something *right*," Kumiko assured him.

Gracefully, she stepped forward with her left foot, humming an accompaniment as she twirled lightly in a full circle, moving her arms smoothly in an arc. Somehow, she'd managed to make this dance step a more successful mimic of the drum than Daniel's awkward karate attempt.

"That looks great," he said in admiration.

"You try," she invited.

"No, I've got two left feet," he protested, realizing too late that he'd just used another expression that she couldn't possibly know. With deep concern, Kumiko looked down at his feet. Daniel couldn't help but laugh.

"No, no, it's just another expression. I'm sorry to confuse you. It just means I'm not a great dancer."

"Well, this is not a great dance. Try." She began humming the melody for him and showing him the step she'd done before. Her long black hair swayed as she moved, catching the last of the sun from the orange twilit sky. She twirled, first to the left, then to the right, her face filled with joy at the movement. This was a dancer. Daniel was enchanted. She reached for his hand to lead him in the dance. Tentatively, he followed. Step forward, foot up, and twirl.

"Good." She nodded. "Now left side." Step forward, foot up, and twirl. Daniel was getting the hang of it.

"Now right," she instructed. He followed. "And . . . turn." They moved in unison. Now, truly enjoying the movement and the nearness of Kumiko, he followed her as she led him dancing through the garden that bordered on the street. They didn't notice others on the street until they heard the applause of a group of little girls, Kumiko's students, admiring their dance, and giggling at the very idea of Kumiko having a boyfriend. A little embarrassed, Daniel bowed to them graciously.

"We're a hit," he told Kumiko. "Maybe we can take the show on the road." He'd done it again.

Kumiko looked at him. "We *are* on the road," she said, pointing to the street where they stood.

There was no explaining that one, so Daniel took her hand and nodded. "Right. Let's try it again, okay?"

Suddenly, the moment was shattered, for there stood Chozen, Taro, and the third young man whose name, Daniel had learned, was Toshio.

Chozen sneered at Daniel as he spoke. "You dance very nice — like a geisha," he teased.

Kumiko tugged at Daniel's hand, trying to lead him from the inevitable trouble. "Come, Daniel-*san*, let's go." But Chozen and his henchmen blocked their way. Daniel's face told the trio nothing, but in his heart he wondered if he'd made the mistake of his life at the vegetable truck with Ichiro. Chozen was looking for a fight. Daniel knew better than to be suckered into it, but he wondered if he could avoid it.

"His teacher's favorite karate technique — the 'let's go' technique," said Chozen. "You know, geisha also sing. You like to sing for us, too?"

"Listen, I'm not looking for any trouble." Daniel tried to appease him.

"Well, maybe trouble is looking for you."

That's what Daniel was worried about. Kumiko spoke to Chozen harshly in Japanese. He snapped back at her in a very surly tone and then turned to Taro. "What's a good American song?"

"Old MacDonald had a farm —"

"Eee, ai, eee, ai, oh . . ." Toshio supplied, laughing at the funny sounds.

"You know it?" Chozen taunted.

"I'm not going to play your game," Daniel told him, taking Kumiko's hand to leave. But Chozen still blocked their way.

"It's not a game. Sing or fight," Chozen challenged, shoving Daniel. Kumiko jumped to his defense, once more rebuking Chozen in Japanese. Toshio pulled her out of the way and restrained her.

"Hey," Daniel protested, going to protect Kumiko.

Chozen shoved him again. "Sing or fight." He spat out the words.

"Cut it out," Daniel urged. But Chozen didn't stop. He shoved Daniel once more and Daniel realized that he'd been pushed to the edge of a steep embankment. There was no more room — another shove and he didn't want to think about the consequences. Chozen's icy stare told him he had to decide. Now.

He charged at Chozen with a well-aimed punch. Chozen sidestepped, evading the punch, and returned with a sharp kick at Danel's stomach. It was right on target. Daniel doubled over in pain, retching from the viciousness of Chozen's kick.

Kumiko ran over to comfort him, but all Daniel could hear was Chozen's threat.

"Next time you insult my honor you are dead." The trio turned and sauntered away. In fury, Kumiko grabbed a tomato that had been abandoned by the roadside and hurled it at Chozen. It splattered on his shoulder, dripping its juices down his back. He turned angrily, but when he saw that Kumiko had thrown it, he merely laughed and walked away.

Kumiko turned her attention to Daniel. "Are you all right?" He stood up slowly, nodding reassuringly to Kumiko. He'd gotten his breath back and was okay, but he was having some trouble understanding Chozen. "I don't get it," he said. "He cheats people and says I'm insulting *his* honor."

"He has no idea what honor is," Kumiko said in disgust.

"I kind of got that feeling."

"Since we were children, he has been the same."

"Well, it can't go on like this." Daniel rubbed his stomach, carefully. "Maybe I can go talk to him. We can work something out."

But Kumiko told him what he already knew: "He will take it as weakness and hurt you again."

"What do you suggest I do?"

"Avoid him," she said, simply.

That sounded a lot like Mr. Miyagi's approach to his problem with Sato. That wasn't working, either.

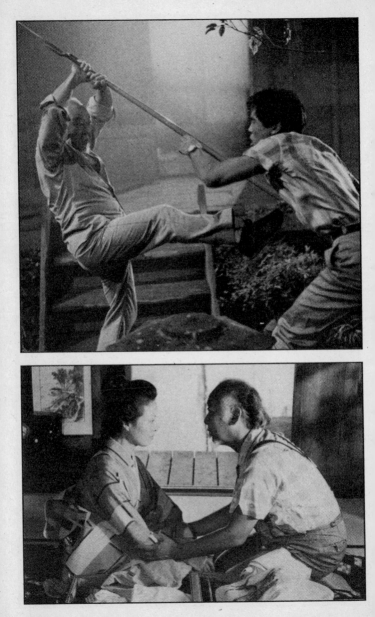

Chapter 10

"Stop, Daniel-*san*. Make no sound," Kumiko whispered to him. They were approaching the gate to Mr. Miyagi's house and there was movement in the light from inside.

Daniel stood next to Kumiko in the shadows of the night and looked in as well. He could see that Mr. Miyagi and Yukie were inside, but he knew Kumiko was right: They were not to be interrupted.

Yukie was wearing an exquisitely embroidered red silk kimono. The wide belt — an *obi* — on her gown was of a rich green silk, tied in an elaborate bow at the back. Mr. Miyagi was also wearing formal Japanese dress, a gray silk kimono trimmed with a red collar and belt. He and Yukie knelt on the floor, facing each other. Between them a low table was laid with plates and cups for tea. It also held a perfectly symmetrical flower arrangement, which somehow seemed to reflect both the joy and the solemnity of the moment. On a brazier next to Yukie, an iron pot was steaming with hot water for tea.

"It's the tea ceremony. We call it *cha no yu*," Kumiko explained, obviously enchanted. Daniel watched as the two people indoors enacted the age-old Japanese ritual. Their motions were so formal, so deliberate, yet so graceful. It was hard to believe he actually knew these people, but he could see that they surely knew each other.

"Your aunt looks beautiful," he told Kumiko.

"She feels beautiful," Kumiko answered.

Yukie bowed to Mr. Miyagi. He bowed to her. Effortlessly, she picked up the steaming pot and poured the water onto the green tea leaves. From outside the window, Daniel and Kumiko watched her perfect preparations; watched her offer the cup to Mr. Miyagi; watched while they proceeded through the ceremony, their eyes never leaving each other.

"What does it mean?" Daniel asked Kumiko.

"It means that they are falling in love again."

The next morning, Daniel was up at dawn to do his karate workout. Once he had finished his exercises, he showered and dressed and then went into the *dojo* and set up a rig that would help him practice the drum technique as he thought he was beginning to understand it. He took a spear from the weapon cabinet and hung it from a beam so it could swing back and forth freely. Standing in front of it, he shoved it away from him and prepared to meet the attack. Just as it nearly reached him, he stepped forward with his left foot for balance and began to twirl, pivoting at the waist, permitting his rising arm and hand to deflect the spear. It worked, but it didn't seem very smooth — or very clever. Moreover, the deflected spear punctured the rice punching bag. The grains of rice sounded like drops of rain when they hit the tatami mat on the floor. Daniel quickly plugged the hole with his finger and looked around for a more permanent solution.

"Daniel-*san*." It was Mr. Miyagi in the garden.

"In here," Daniel told him, panicked about the rice sack. Thinking fast, he jammed a stick of gum in his mouth to soften it. Three rapid chews and he extracted the gum and covered the rip with it. He just had time to turn the sack around when Mr. Miyagi came into the *dojo*.

"Good morning. How was your date last night?" he asked his teacher.

"Very nice. What are you doing?" he asked, examining the spear.

"Experimenting. Want to see something?" Mr. Miyagi nodded.

Daniel flexed his knees, crouching into a fighting position, and then pivoted, swinging his arms as Kumiko had taught him.

"How's that?"

Mr. Miyagi nodded approval. "Very good, Daniel-*san*. Now use hips for power."

Mr. Miyagi demonstrated what he meant about his hips and Daniel followed. He understood how the movement Mr. Miyagi suggested would add strength to the maneuver. Perhaps he *could* unravel the secret of the drum — with a little help from his friends.

He began dismantling the rig he'd made for

the spear and replaced the spear on the weapon rack.

"Kumiko's going to take me on a tour around the island today. If it's okay with you."

"Fine," Mr. Miyagi agreed. "We'll meet in Naha City after. I must go there to change house title. I am giving it to Yukie."

"You still love her, don't you?" Daniel asked.

"*Hai.*"

"You could do worse. I mean, I don't know her that well, but you can just tell the kind of person she is. Look how long she waited. Took care of things for your father and not to mention that she's a great cook." Daniel was getting caught up in his own enthusiasm. "I mean, if you like that kind of food."

"Daniel-*san.*"

"Yes?"

"Use hips, not lips."

Then came the sound of gentle rain, but it wasn't rain. It was rice. Before Daniel could start to explain, they were interrupted by Kumiko's cheery greeting: "*Ohayo!*"

Mr. Miyagi glanced at the rice bag and then at Daniel. "More advice," he said. "Don't keep ladies waiting. Have a good time," he said, dismissing Daniel.

Daniel and Kumiko happily left together, but before they went through the gate, Daniel glanced over his shoulder to see Mr. Miyagi removing the gum and placing a patch over the hole in the bag. He was smiling.

Daniel took Kumiko's hand. "Okay, now, I'm ready for the Cook's tour."

He'd done it again.

"Cook's tour? I don't cook. Are you cook? I thought you are a student. . . ."

"I'm sorry, Kumiko. It's just an expression, you see . . ." he began.

Chapter 11

Daniel surveyed the breathtaking view in front of him. He stood with Kumiko on a hill overlooking the sea. To their left, on a cliff at the ocean's edge, the ruins of an ancient castle guarded the shore. Parts of the wall had crumbled, but the main section of the fortress and most of the buildings within its walls still stood. It was not hard to imagine this place manned by medieval Japanese warriors, fierce in black lacquered leather armor.

"These are the ruins of the Castle of King Shohashi," Kumiko explained.

"The Peace King," Daniel supplied, recalling it from his book about Okinawa.

"You know King Shohashi?"

"Not personally," he joked. Kumiko laughed, too.

"Name of castle in Japanese is Castle of Courtesy and Good Manners."

"Why is it called that?"

"See over there?" She pointed to her right toward the horizon. "China. And there —" She pointed to her left. "Japan. We on Okinawa live between giants. Best way to survive is by having courtesy and good manners. King Shohashi built the castle here to always remind us. Every summer for eight hundred years Bon dance is held here. But no more."

"Why?"

"Sato," she said in explanation. Then added, "He sells it. Piece by piece."

"To whom?" Daniel asked.

"Collectors. Museums. Anyone with money." She sighed.

"Bet old King Shohashi wouldn't be too happy about that."

"No one is. This is our history."

"Why doesn't anybody say something about it?"

"Not everyone with ears can hear," Kumiko explained.

"Maybe you should talk louder." But somehow that answer seemed too simple in this complex land. "Say, can we go over to the castle?"

Kumiko nodded, her eyes lighting up. "Oh, yes. Legend is, if you race to the castle and win, your wish will come true."

"You want a head start?" Daniel offered gallantly.

"Not necessary, thank you. Ready?"

Daniel crouched in a runner's starting position. "Yep. I'm ready."

"Set?"

"Yes, I'm —" He was interrupted by her departure. She flew past him toward the castle, yelling, "Go!" when she was a dozen steps ahead of him. Laughing, he started running after her. He caught up only to be bumped aside by her on a sharp turn. By the time he caught up again, she was ahead of him on the stairs and wouldn't let him past her. Triumphantly, she crested the top of the stairs and raised her hands in victory.

"I won," she announced.

"You cheated," Daniel told her.

"Okay, then," she agreed. "We'll share the wish. Close your eyes." He did.

Suddenly, he was very aware of her closeness. He opened his eyes and looked into hers. His happiness was reflected in her face, which was tilted up to him. She came closer, and then —

"*Soko ni iru no wa donata desu ka!?*" (Who is there!?) came the gruff, unwelcome voice of the castle watchman. Kumiko put her finger to her lips and led Daniel down the other side of the wall to tour the rest of the castle.

Four hours later, Kumiko's island tour brought Daniel to Okinawa's main city, Naha. Once again he was struck by the meeting of East and West in this city. The streets were jammed with cars and motorcycles, pedicabs maneuvering around jeeps, while people crowded the sidewalks. Asian and Western faces mingled easily — uniforms and short haircuts identifying the U.S. military personnel. Street vendors sold their wares, laid out on sheets on the sidewalk, offering everything from chopsticks to copper-topped batteries.

Daniel stared at the strange mixture of cultures, enjoying it. Kumiko had ducked into the video store, next to the traditional teahouse, around the corner from the video arcade, across the street from the sushi bar. He didn't mind her leaving him for a few minutes. There was plenty to look at and even after she joined him again, he continued to watch the dramas of the street. She was watching the video in the window of the store.

It caught Daniel's eye, too, and he turned to watch with her, fascinated to hear Laurence Olivier perfectly at ease, speaking flawless Japanese as the soundtrack of *Wuthering Heights* blared through the shop's loudspeaker. While Olivier's Heathcliff was gearing up in the big love scene, Daniel was finding it harder to keep from laughing at the strangeness of his Japanese, but Kumiko was spellbound, near tears.

"Do you like this?" he asked, a little surprised.

"My favorite film," she answered, leaving him more confused. He shrugged and changed the subject.

"What tape did you get?" he asked, pointing to the bag she held.

"Modern dance." She displayed the cassette she'd bought.

"You go to school for it?"

Woefully, Kumiko shook her head. "No schools for this in Okinawa."

"Too bad."

"Doesn't matter," Kumiko said with resignation. But Daniel knew she didn't mean it. Even from the little he'd seen her dance, he knew she was good — very good — and he knew it had to be hard for her to live in a place where she couldn't get any training. He thought about how hard it would have been for him to learn karate from a video tape. Probably the luckiest day of his life was the day he'd met Mr. Miyagi — though it hadn't seemed that way at the time.

Just then, they were interrupted by a young boy who was cutting through the crowd, handing out fliers to everyone. *"Dozo, dozo,"* he said, *Please, please,* shoving the paper at passersby. Kumiko took one from him and her eyes lit up.

"What's it say?" Daniel asked.

"Rock 'n' roll dancing tomorrow night. Want to go?"

"Oh, sure. That'd be fun, I guess," he answered, but something else had caught his attention. He looked across the street at a double storefront plate glass window. In English, the sign read: WORLD HEADQUARTERS — MASTER SATO — OKINAWAN KARATE. When Kumiko saw the sign, she tugged at Daniel's arm, trying to distract him.

"Must meet Miyagi-*san* and my aunt."

"I just want to look —"

"Daniel-*san*. Remember what I said," she cautioned him.

"It's a public street. There are lots of people around. Nothing's going to happen." He stepped across the street, and stared into the plate glass. Inside, he could see about sixty men — all American GI's. They were taking a class. Each in turn was attacking Chozen or Taro. Each in turn was beaten by Chozen or Taro. Daniel shook his head in frank admiration.

"Where do the Okinawans study?" he asked.

"Where they can learn real karate."

"What is this?"

"We call this *business* karate."

"Having the Americans here really changed things for your people, didn't it?"

"And for your people, too," Kumiko shrugged and smiled in answer. She and Daniel found themselves watching a young American soldier and his Okinawan wife, their Okinawan/American baby perched on his father's shoulders, eating an ice-cream cone.

"Come, Daniel-*san*. Time to meet Miyagi-*san* and Auntie Yukie."

"*Hai,*" he answered.

Chapter 12

"KIIIIAIIIII!" . . . Thonk! Crash! . . . "Aaaargh! Ooowh!"

Daniel and Kumiko stopped to listen. The anguished cry of pain was followed by applause mingled with raucous laughter and then loud chattering. As they stood by the door of a building near the place they were to meet Mr. Miyagi and Yukie, Daniel and Kumiko watched a young American soldier emerge, his swollen hand cradled in a towel.

Daniel looked at the building more carefully. It was a bar, complete with video games and pool tables, as well as other diversions obviously designed to separate the American soldiers from their paychecks. It was the sort of place his mother used to rush him past. Right now, however, it seemed almost irresistible.

"KIIIIAIIIII!" Another loud thunk followed by a roar of pain, and then laughter.

"We're going to be late," Kumiko warned him.

"Come on," Daniel said, leading her inside.

"Daniel-*san*, please."

He pulled her into the dark and smoky room, lit by the flashing lights from the video games. They walked toward the rear, crossing paths with another American soldier protecting his broken hand in a towel. Finally, they reached the source of the noise.

What they found were four sawhorses holding a wooden plank. On the plank three one-inch slabs of ice were stacked on top of each other, spaced an inch apart. Shattered ice and pools of water littered the floor and the makeshift table. The crowd chattered wildly, exchanging agreement on bets, watching a muscular American soldier, stripped to the waist, as he rolled his shoulder, warming up. His buddies, standing by, each held wads of cash in their hands. The betting had obviously been active.

The American moved in front of the ice slabs and flexed his knees in a classic karate stance.

"Quiet! Quiet everybody!"

The man took a few measured trial swings and then four deep breaths. It didn't look right to Daniel.

"He's not going to do it," he whispered to Kumiko. But the whisper distracted the man, who glowered at Daniel and then began his ritual again. With more fury than force he yelled "Kiiiaiiii!" and chopped at the blocks. His hand cut through two cakes of ice, but was stopped by the third. His *kiiaii* turned to a howl of pain. Someone gave him a towel and, in disgust and humiliation, he headed for the door.

"Told you," Daniel said to Kumiko.

"He looked very strong."

"You have to be strong here —" He tapped his head. "Not here —" He tapped his bicep. "See, that's what Mr. Miyagi was teach —"

"Think you could do better, big mouth?" the soldier asked him.

Daniel took Kumiko's arm to leave the place. "Couldn't do worse," he said, bragging more than he really felt he ought. He turned to leave, but suddenly he found himself facing Chozen, Toshio, and Taro. Somehow, the word had gotten to them that Daniel was here.

"Let's see about that," Chozen challenged.

Daniel was getting a bad feeling about this.

"Maybe some other time," he tried.

"There is no other time," Chozen told him.

"Listen, whatever problems Mr. Miyagi has with your uncle — it's between them. There don't have to be problems between *us*," Daniel reasoned.

"No. We have our own."

Suddenly, Kumiko, her face etched in fear, dropped Daniel's hand and darted through the crowd to the door. Chozen watched her leave and then turned to his henchmen.

"Taro, you call my uncle. Toshio, you take bets."

With a sinking feeling, Daniel realized that what had started out as a lark, a glimpse at a sideshow, was about to turn into a nightmare. He was going to be the main attraction at the sideshow. There was no way out of it.

Chozen spoke to a few of the soldiers and Daniel knew the word was getting around.

"Hey, listen here," one of the GI's announced. "We got a real live stateside karate champ."

The betting started.

"I give three to one!" Chozen announced. The betting was vigorous.

"I'm not going to do it," Daniel told Chozen.

Chozen smiled at him coldly. "You have a choice — broken ice or broken neck. Understand?" One look at Chozen's eyes and Daniel knew he meant it.

"He gotta break all three?" one of the soldiers asked.

"No," Chozen said. "Just one. Three to one says he can't do that."

Sato appeared at the edge of the crowd and watched while the fresh ice cakes were stacked. The crowd became more and more excited at the prospect and the tension built as the noise grew. Daniel barely heard it, though. All he had in his mind were the images of the defeated GI's cradling their injured hands in white towels. Daniel was near panic.

"All bets in?" the loud American asked.

"No!" The voice was forceful. It was familiar. Heads craned to see who the new bettor was. It was Mr. Miyagi.

"Boy, am I glad you're here," said Daniel.

"Don't worry. Miyagi fix everything." What sweet words, Daniel thought. But then Mr. Miyagi asked, "What are the odds?"

The American answered, "Three to one he doesn't make it through even one piece of ice."

Mr. Miyagi took out his wallet and removed all the cash from it.

"Four hundred dollars," he said, glancing at the bills. "He breaks all three."

Chozen blanched. "I cannot cover it," he said. There was a moment of suspended animation in the bar. Then a hand slammed down on the table, covering a stack of money. It was Sato.

"You are covered," he told Mr. Miyagi.

Daniel couldn't believe this was happening.

"Wait a second," he said. He took Mr. Miyagi aside. "Great. Now what do I do?" he asked his teacher.

"Focus. It's all our money."

"And what are you going to do?"

"Pray."

Daniel watched in amazement while Mr. Miyagi clasped his hands together in a prayer position and then gave Daniel a knowing look.

Then Daniel knew. While the crowd chanted, "Let's go, let's go, let's go," Daniel calmly stepped up to the ice. He looked at his hands and put them together. He inhaled and then exhaled, raising his hands high above his head. Inhale, down again. Exhaling, he reached forward. Inhale, he returned his hands to the prayer position. He could feel the healing, calming power of his breath. He could focus. He repeated the exercise, and again, until every cell in his body was focused on the ice in front of him. Easily, he inhaled a final time and with the exhale, he swung his right hand down at the ice. Smoothly, his hand sliced through all three blocks and came to rest unharmed on the wooden plank.

The crowd began yelling in frenzied admiration for Daniel's feat and was screaming at Chozen for their money. He paid out his bets, mouth agape. Calmly, Mr. Miyagi reached for Sato's money and grasped it. Before he could pick it up, however, Chozen's hand slammed down on top of his.

"We do not honor bets with cowards," he spat out at Mr. Miyagi.

Sato glared at his nephew angrily. "Do not embarrass me with the same mistake twice," he chastised. Chozen removed his hand from the money. Mr. Miyagi, Daniel, and Kumiko cut through the crowd and exited to the street.

When they got to the corner, Mr. Miyagi paused to count his cash.

"How could you do that to me?" Daniel demanded.

"Two hundred, two fifty, three hundred. . . ." He paused. "You do it to yourself, Daniel-*san*. Three fifty, four hundred —"

"I suppose, but you could have helped me a little."

"I did."

"Yeah, how?" he challenged.

"Won your college tuition," he said, handing Daniel a roll of cash. "Now, come. Miyagi has work to do. Tomorrow is tomato harvest. Unless you want to stay in town. . . ."

Pocketing the money, Daniel glanced over his shoulder. There, at the door to the bar, stood Chozen and his henchmen.

"Let's go see the tomatoes," Daniel said, and they began walking to the parking lot.

How did he know I could do it? Daniel wondered. Did he know I could do it? If he didn't know I could do it, how could he have bet every cent we have? And how could he be so cool about it? The questions were unanswered — and unanswerable. Mr. Miyagi was Mr. Miyagi and there was nobody else like him. Perhaps that was a good thing, Daniel thought, feeling the thick roll of bills in his pocket.

Chapter 13

The next afternoon, Daniel was tidying the Miyagi *dojo* after his own workout. Once again, he was drawn by the weapon collection and was dusting it meticulously with a handkerchief he'd found on the shelf. When he'd finished dusting, he dropped the handkerchief in the wastebasket.

"Thought you had a date." Mr. Miyagi spoke from the door.

"I do, but I figured I'd clean up a little while I was waiting."

"Very good," Mr. Miyagi said approvingly. "But don't throw away weapons," he chastised, plucking the dusty handkerchief from the trash.

"Oh, yeah," Daniel joked. "The old sneeze-blocker, right? That's what my grandfather used to call it."

Mr. Miyagi dropped the handkerchief on the floor at his feet. "Pick up," he instructed.

Daniel bent down to retrieve it.

"Now look up," Mr. Miyagi told him.

Daniel looked up at his teacher from his crouched position.

"What do you see?" Mr. Miyagi asked.

Daniel realized that what he was actually looking at was Mr. Miyagi's groin. He struggled for a polite description.

"Umm . . . your, uhhh. . . ."

"Primary target good enough," Mr. Miyagi supplied. Of course it was true. Daniel realized that the crouching position was an excellent one from which to launch an attack that would completely take the fight out of an opponent. It wasn't the sort of karate you could or would use in a tournament, but in Okinawa he was learning that karate wasn't really intended for tournaments. For some people, it was a way of life.

"That's pretty neat." Daniel smiled approvingly, replacing the handkerchief on the weapons rack. "Thanks. I hope I won't need to use it."

"*Konban wa!* Good evening," Kumiko interrupted politely, entering the *dojo*. Daniel and Mr. Miyagi turned to her and both bowed. She held two shopping bags, one in each hand. She offered one to Daniel. "This is for you."

"What is it?"

"Dance clothes. Try on," she explained.

"Dance clothes?" he asked, confused.

"*Hai.*"

Before he could ask further, they were interrupted again by the harsh, familiar voice of Chozen, calling from the garden.

"Miyagi! Miyagi!" he yelled rudely.

When they reached the garden, they saw, with dismay, that Chozen, Taro, and Toshio were grouped in the middle of the vegetable patch, holding large hoes. Chozen's shouts had attracted many of the villagers, who gathered at the gate of the garden to watch the confrontation.

Chozen spoke. "My uncle says his obligation to your father's memory is fulfilled. He waits at his *dojo*. I have been sent to get you."

"Tell him I am a farmer, not a fighter," Mr. Miyagi responded.

On a signal from Chozen, Toshio and Taro began slashing at the radish garden with their hoes. Within seconds, the destruction was complete.

"Now farming is finished," Chozen announced.

Without answering, Mr. Miyagi bent down and began to clear the patch of the ruined radishes.

"What are you doing?" Chozen demanded.

"Replanting," Mr. Miyagi said simply.

In frustrated fury, Chozen kicked dirt in the old man's face, but Mr. Miyagi would not be distracted from his chore. One by one, the villagers joined him, helping him to prepare the Miyagi garden for planting.

Disgusted, Chozen, Taro, and Toshio abandoned the ruined garden and stalked to their car. Daniel could barely hear the squeal of the tires over the monotonous cadence of the farmers' tools.

When the patch was cleared, Mr. Miyagi told his friends he would plant it by himself. The neighbors left, and Daniel and Kumiko went into the house to ready themselves for the dance. Daniel was still curious about the dance clothes Kumiko had brought him.

He emptied the shopping bag on the floor and laughed to find a pair of fifties blue jeans, pegged at the bottom, a garish Hawaiian shirt to be worn over a white T-shirt that would show at the neck above the open collar, a pair of Cuban heeled shoes with pointy toes, and white athletic socks. For accessories, there were a wide brown leather belt with a Western buckle and a denim jacket.

Kumiko was changing her clothes in the adjoining room so they could chat easily through the paper walls. Daniel's thoughts were of Mr. Miyagi.

"You think they're going to fight?" he asked Kumiko.

"No," she answered.

"Why not?"

"Because Miyagi-*san* is a great man."

Her feeling about Mr. Miyagi surprised Daniel. "Even though he ran out on your aunt?"

"Didn't run. Chose to go," she explained.

"What's the difference?"

"Principles."

"Don't you think there is something sad about that?" he asked.

"*Hai*. But also very romantic."

Her comment reminded Daniel of her tears at the movie *Wuthering Heights*. Were Mr. Miyagi and Yukie really another Heathcliff and Cathy?

"Sounds like the stories where everyone is in love, but no one lives happily ever after," he said.

"Exactly like. We call them happy-sad stories."

"I like happy-happy myself," Daniel told her.

"Ah, but life is not like that," she warned.

"I like to think it can be," Daniel said.

"Ready," she answered. The door between them slid open.

He couldn't help laughing when he saw Kumiko. The small, fragile Okinawan flower was garbed in the outfit of a 1955 rock 'n' roll beauty queen. She was wearing black velvet toreador pants with a halter top that showed a bare midriff. On her feet were a pair of fur-trimmed spike heels, which made her three inches taller. Her hair was pulled back into a bobbing pony tail, bangs in front, plastic barrettes on the sides.

Her eyes lit up when she saw Daniel. She produced a tube of gooey hair cream and applied it to Daniel's head, pompadouring his hair into a fifties hairstyle.

"Don't you think we're going to stand out?" he asked, a little uncertain about his costume.

"Lucky if we get noticed at all," she replied. "Eat your heart out, James Dean. Right, Daniel-*san*?"

"Sure thing, Annette!"

Why not? he asked himself.

Kumiko was absolutely right. Their costumes were unexceptional in the crowd at the dance. Everyone had found old clothes to wear, most of them a good deal wilder than Daniel and Kumiko's. Once his self-consciousness was gone, Daniel could settle down and just have a good time with Kumiko. In fact, Daniel was finding it very easy to have a good time with Kumiko.

"How do you like it?" Kumiko asked, waving her hand to indicate the oddly attired crowd and golden oldies music.

"Wild," he answered.

"Can you dance to this music?" she asked.

"I can try," he said, taking her hand and leading her to the dance floor. The amplifiers were blasting out "Rock Around the Clock," and Daniel found that he could easily pick up the essential movements of the lindy hop. Soon Daniel was relaxed and having a great time. He saw that Kumiko's face glowed with happiness, reflecting his own feelings.

When the song ended, they slipped off the dance floor and over to the refreshment table. Daniel fetched two sodas and handed one to Kumiko.

"Can I ask you something personal?" he asked as they sank onto the folding chairs.

"Yes."

"Do you have a boyfriend?"

"No. Do you have a girl friend?"

"I did," he answered, thinking about Ali for the first time since he'd left California.

"What happened?" Kumiko asked, sensing Daniel's sadness.

"We broke up," he explained.

"Why?"

"You know, I'm not really sure."

"Does that happen a lot in America?" Kumiko asked.

"That people break up?" he said, confused.

"No. That you don't know why."

"I don't know. I don't have that much experience in the field," he answered truthfully, standing up and holding out his hand to invite her to dance. Johnny Mathis was singing "Chances Are."

"Me, neither," she shrugged, joining him on the dance floor.

Daniel encircled Kumiko with his arms, dancing slowly with the music, feeling her cheek next to his, her arms around his waist, her feet in step with his. There on the dance floor, they seemed alone. There were no California, no Ali, no Mr. Miyagi, no Sato, no Chozen. There were just Daniel and Kumiko.

But not for long.

Suddenly, Daniel felt a sharp rap on his shoulder. He turned and found himself facing Chozen, Taro, and Toshio. This trio had developed the bad habit of showing up when things were going smoothly for Daniel.

"What do you want from me now?" Daniel demanded.

"My money back — for starters," Chozen said with a cold challenge.

"I won it fairly," Daniel protested.

Before Daniel knew what was happening, Chozen's fist darted out and struck him sharply in the stomach, knocking the wind out of him. Surprised, Daniel doubled over in pain. As quickly as Chozen had doubled him over, he was straightened up by Toshio while Taro grabbed Kumiko from behind and held his hand over her mouth. Chozen plunged his hand into Daniel's pocket, retrieving the winnings Mr. Miyagi had given him.

"That's all my money," Daniel protested. Smirking, Chozen peeled two bills off the roll and dropped them on the floor at his feet. Automatically, Daniel crouched and picked them up. Then he glanced up at Chozen, realizing with a start that he was staring at what Mr. Miyagi had called a primary target area. In an instant, Daniel attacked. He delivered a single sharp punch to Chozen and Chozen fell to the floor in agony. While Daniel retrieved his money from Chozen's fist, Kumiko ground her spike heel into Taro's instep and pushed him into Toshio. Daniel grabbed Kumiko's hand and the two of them fled into the night from the disabled trio on the dance floor.

As they drove home, Daniel thought about the confrontation. It was the end of another round, and, as with some of the previous ones, it had gone to Daniel, but he knew it wasn't the last round, and he doubted that he would win them all. He had the very uneasy feeling that things were going to get worse before they got better. Chozen was not, after all, a cake of ice that could be broken with a focused blow or would melt to nothing in defeat. Not at all.

Daniel was still deep in thought when Kumiko's car drew up to Mr. Miyagi's house.

"Don't say anything about what happened, okay?" he asked.

Kumiko nodded.

Daniel moved over in the front seat. He was just beginning to think that it might be a good idea to kiss Kumiko good-night when Yukie came up to the car.

"Miyagi-*san* has gone fishing," she told them. "You come stay our house?"

It was tempting to go to the protection of Yukie's house, but Daniel knew that his job was to stay with his friend. He suspected Mr. Miyagi would need him and he should be there. Over protests from both Yukie and Kumiko, he went into Mr. Miyagi's house alone, after bowing good-night politely to the women. He heard the car drive away. The night was quiet.

Daniel stepped out into the backyard, which overlooked the lagoon. In the center of the lagoon, he saw a boat. Mr. Miyagi sat motionless in the boat, he and his fishing rod silhouetted by the moon.

Somehow, it didn't seem right to Daniel to sleep in the house without Mr. Miyagi there. He went instead into the *dojo*. Glancing around at the family portrait gallery, he invited himself in.

"You guys mind if I sleep here?"

No answer.

"Didn't think you would."

He rolled out a mat to sleep on, covering himself with a *gi* jacket. As an afterthought, he rose and walked to the weapons rack, retrieving a spear. He placed it next to his mat and lay down to sleep. Uneasily.

Chapter 14

Daniel awoke as uneasily as he had slept. He sat upright suddenly. The noise of glass breaking and wood snapping shattered his sleep as well. Grabbing the spear that still lay at his side, he jumped up and ran out into the garden where the noise came from.

"Where is Miyagi?" Sato's booming voice demanded, cutting through the early morning fog.

"I don't know," Daniel told him, wondering to himself about the source of the destructive noises. His question was answered when Chozen, Taro, and Toshio appeared from around the corner, near the greenhouse. Daniel dreaded to think what damage they had done.

"He is not here, Uncle," Chozen reported to Sato.

Sato scowled in acknowledgment, turned, and left the garden. Over his shoulder, he muttered the order, "Destroy the garden."

With murderous glee, Toshio and Taro began ripping apart the beautiful contemplative garden that had been planted and tended by generations of Miyagis. They stepped on the ancient bonsai trees, breaking their branches, and then tore their roots from the ground.

In fury, Daniel attacked them with the spear. But before he reached the nearest one, Chozen stuck his foot out and Daniel tripped over it, tumbling into the dirt and losing his grip on the spear. Taro ran over to attack, but while he was in midleap, Daniel grasped his ankles with a reverse scissor clasp, arresting Taro's flight with a decisive thud. Daniel finished with a sharp punch to the back of Taro's neck and then scrambled to his spear, lying just out of reach. Taro rose shakily and sprang to the side of his cohorts.

With the spear in his hand, Daniel leaped to his feet and used the weapon to hold the three attackers at bay. The three spread out, Chozen in front of Daniel, flanked by his henchmen who now held the damaged bonsai as weapons. They taunted Daniel with them, feinting to the left and right, trying to confuse him. Chozen smiled at him in icy amusement.

"What are you going to do what that, little coward?" he said, pointing to the spear.

"Come and find out," Daniel challenged.

"I will."

With that, Chozen attacked. Quickly countering, Daniel lunged at Chozen with the spear. Chozen slipped to the right and ducked underneath the unwieldy weapon, coming up behind Daniel. He wrested the spear from Daniel's hands and began to use it to choke Daniel. Daniel could feel his air supply cut off by the deadly weapon and flailed frantically trying to remove it from his throat. No matter how he moved, he couldn't budge Chozen.

"This is your teacher's fault," Chozen sputtered. "If he were a man with honor, you would live. But he's not."

With that, Chozen bore down with the spear. Daniel couldn't get out of the hold. He was becoming weaker, almost unconscious, almost beyond caring. There seemed to be no end. No help. Nothing.

Suddenly, through his blurred vision, Daniel saw a figure. It reminded him of a scene long ago near a chain-link fence. Daniel struggled to remember. The figure attacked his attackers. A kick to Toshio's neck; a deadly punch at Taro's stomach; and snap kick follow-up to Taro; a roundhouse punch at Toshio. Chozen's henchmen stumbled and fell. Then, as suddenly as the pressure on Daniel's neck had begun, it ended. Chozen released him, pushing Daniel aside to fight the attacker. Daniel gasped for air, desperate to fill his starving lungs. Then he looked up.

It was Mr. Miyagi. Somehow, Daniel wasn't surprised. He had first seen that fighting stance at the Halloween Dance at his high school the night Johnny and his friends from the Cobra Kai Karate Dojo had nearly killed Daniel. Mr. Miyagi had saved his life then; he was doing so again now.

Chozen grabbed the spear and turned to Mr. Miyagi, charging straight at him with all his force. A second before it would pierce him with deadly force, Mr. Miyagi turned, grasping the spear with both hands, instantly stopping Chozen's charge.

Mr. Miyagi lifted the spear, raising Chozen off the ground and spinning him in the air. In terror, Chozen released his own grasp of the spear and came crashing to the ground. Mr. Miyagi stood motionless over Chozen, the lethal point of the spear directed at Chozen's throat. In a moment, Chozen would be dead — or alive — at Mr. Miyagi's whim.

The old man withdrew the spear from Chozen's throat and easily snapped the long weapon in two over his knee. He tossed the halves aside.

Chozen sprang to his feet and looked at his attacker defiantly: "The act of a coward!" He spat on the ground and strode out of the garden as if victory were his. Toshio and Taro trailed after him sheepishly.

"Are you all right, Daniel-*san*?" Mr. Miyagi asked.

Daniel nodded, barely able to speak. But he was alive, he could breathe, he was all right.

Just then, Yukie and Kumiko came into the garden, and stood by the gate, stunned by the devastation. Mr. Miyagi barely saw them. He went to look at the plants Chozen had destroyed. Daniel and the women watched while he stroked a branch of one of the ancient bonsai, now reduced to splinters. His face tightened into a mask of anger and resolution.

"Stay here," he told Daniel and headed to the gate.

"Where are you going?" Daniel rasped.

"To put an end to this." He left the garden.

"Mr. Miyagi, wait!" But he didn't wait. Daniel heard the car door slam and the engine turn over.

He stood up and ran to the garden gate, too.

"Miyagi-*san* said to stay," Kumiko said, but Daniel stepped around her through the gate to see the receding taillights of the car. He turned to Kumiko.

"Will you take me in your car?"

"I can't."

"Then give me the keys."

"You don't know the road."

Daniel was desperate. He had to convince Kumiko to help him.

"Listen, you don't understand. I've got to help him."

Kumiko hesitated, but then opened the door to her car and got in. Quickly, Daniel climbed in on the other side and they followed Mr. Miyagi.

Daniel was afraid of what would happen when Mr. Miyagi met Sato. He had to make sure he was there with him.

"Hurry, Kumiko," he urged her. She nodded and continued to follow Mr. Miyagi's car.

They caught up with Mr. Miyagi in Naha City. At first Daniel was confused, because Mr. Miyagi's car wasn't parked anywhere near Sato's *dojo*. Then, in dismay, he realized, glancing at the building across the sidewalk, that Mr. Miyagi had gone to a travel agency. He had gotten reservations to go back to the U.S., Daniel guessed. He jumped out of the car and caught Mr. Miyagi on the sidewalk.

"You're leaving," he accused.

"*We*'re leaving," Mr. Miyagi corrected him.

"The house is completely wrecked."

"Houses can be repaired," Mr. Miyagi said.

"And what about three-hundred-year-old trees?" Daniel asked, hoping to touch the old man's feelings.

"Trees can be replanted."

"And dirt comes off your face with a little soap and water?" Daniel challenged sarcastically.

"You're learning," Mr. Miyagi told him.

Daniel couldn't understand Mr. Miyagi saying these things. Sure, he would go a long way to avoid a fight, but Daniel couldn't have imagined that it would come to Mr. Miyagi *running* from a fight. Going home now really was the act of a coward. Nothing was resolved and nothing ever could be resolved if they left.

"You know," Daniel began. "I don't get something. When I had my problem with Johnny and those other jerks, you told me to stand up to them."

"Told you to face reality," Mr. Miyagi corrected.

"What about you facing it?"

"I am."

"No, you're not. You're running away," he said.

"Do you think I am afraid, Daniel-*san*?" he asked.

Did he? Daniel looked at his friend, confused about everything — not knowing what was true, what was a lie.

"It's been a difficult time, Daniel. Come home. Rest," Mr. Miyagi said softly.

Daniel wasn't ready to go. He had to think. He had to try to understand.

"I'm not tired. I'll see you later."

He turned and walked away. Alone. Very alone.

Chapter 15

Naha City seemed only a series of splashes of color to Daniel. He wandered aimlessly, lost in thought, completely unaware of his surroundings. He didn't hear the blaring traffic; he didn't see the crowds of people.

He inhaled deeply and focused.

A lie becomes the truth only if you believe it. So what was the lie? Most important: What was the truth?

Mr. Miyagi wasn't afraid. He wasn't afraid of anything — certainly not of Sato. If he could take on three of Sato's students at once, he could take on Sato. So why wouldn't he? The lie was that Mr. Miyagi was a coward. And the truth? Daniel didn't know; he wasn't sure. He was pretty sure that the answer didn't lie on an airplane back to the U.S. But he knew that if Mr. Miyagi fought Sato, one of them wouldn't walk away.

Daniel stood motionless on the sidewalk for a long time, staring, without seeing, at the window of a store. Suddenly, his eyes focused on the window. It was an Army-Navy surplus store. The windows were full of weapons: guns, rifles, bayonets — the machined tools of modern warfare — a sharp contrast to the implements — and handkerchief — on the weapon shelf in the Miyagi *dojo*.

Daniel walked into the store.

To his right was a large open display case full of firearms. Two young American soldiers were rummaging through the secondhand weapons. One of them hefted an M-60, Rambo style.

"How much?" asked one of the soldiers.

The salesman scurried over to the customers.

"Vietnam original," he assured them, nodding sagely. "Two hundred dollars. Good buy. And," he said, retrieving a small metal device from his pocket and pointing at the absent firing pin on the M-60, "for ten dollars more, converts to live ammo." He smiled again.

The soldier aimed the M-60 at a field full of imaginary enemies. His buddy picked up an M-79 grenade launcher, snapped it open, mimed loading it, slammed it closed, and aimed high. With his lips, he imitated the peculiarly mild popping sound the launcher would make when firing its deadly ammunition. His friend tugged at the harmless trigger of the M-60 and blew away the field of VC before him. The scene reminded Daniel of nothing so much as two little boys playing war games. But there was something eerie about the harmless deadly weapons — the truth, but a lie.

The salesman broke into their game. "Sale on forty-fives," he told them.

"No, thanks," they said, tossing their weapons back into the bin and leaving empty-handed.

Daniel watched them go and then began looking at the weapons in the store. Suddenly, one of the display cases caught his eye and he walked over to it, focusing. The case held a cardboard box full of military medals.

"I help you?" The eager salesman shuffled to the case.

"Yeah. How much is that one?" he asked, pointing to the familiar medal, just like Mr. Miyagi's. The Congressional Medal of Honor.

The salesman retrieved it from the jumble in the box.

"Ah, good choice," he told Daniel approvingly. "Medal of Honor. One owner. Just one."

Daniel held it in his hand, turning it over, studying it. What was the magic of it? What did it mean? What could it tell him?

"Fifty dollar," the salesman said.

"Is it real?"

"Real, real," the man nodded, vigorously.

Sure it was real, but it was just a piece of cloth and a chunk of metal. Then Daniel understood. It wasn't the medal that mattered. The medal without honor and principles was meaningless. In fact, the only things that mattered were honor and principles. To fail to understand that was to mistake a couple of young soldiers playing with harmless guns for heroes; was to mistake Sato's belligerent bravura for honor.

Fighting Sato, even beating him, would prove nothing for or about Mr. Miyagi. The only way

Mr. Miyagi could overcome Sato was to uphold his own principles and the surest way to lose them was to fight Sato.

That was the truth.

"Okay, for you, thirty-five dollar," the salesman sputtered, mistaking Daniel's thoughtfulness for hesitation. Daniel shook his head, putting the medal down on the counter. He looked up and saw Mr. Miyagi standing in the store. Daniel knew he'd watched the whole thing.

"Fighting is the easy way out, isn't it?" Daniel asked him softly.

"Much easier," Mr. Miyagi agreed, smiling at Daniel's understanding.

"I guess we should go home and pack."

"*Hai.*"

They walked out of the store together.

"Okay. Okay. Fifteen dollar! Last price." The salesman trailed after them.

They didn't turn around.

Chapter 16

Daniel lowered the lid of his suitcase and snapped it closed. He glanced out the window of his loft and saw Kumiko sitting by the pond, solemnly tossing rice into the water. In a way, it was going to be very hard for him to leave Okinawa.

On his way out to join Kumiko, Daniel passed Mr. Miyagi's room where Yukie was helping him to pack his things. Daniel didn't mean to eavesdrop — nor did he want to interrupt. He stood quietly on the stairs near the door, out of sight.

"Come with me," Mr. Miyagi said, speaking to Yukie.

"I cannot," she answered.

"What is here to keep you?"

"My whole life."

"So we will build a new one," he invited.

"The time to build is when you are young."

"If I could stay, I would," Mr. Miyagi said.

"If I could go, I would," she told him.

Daniel slipped past the door, and out to the garden to talk to Kumiko.

She was poised on an outcropping of black rock

that jutted over the water. She held a bowl of raw rice in one hand; with the other, she scattered grains on the water.

"Hi," Daniel said.

"Hi."

"What are you doing?"

"Old custom," she told him. "When fishermen would go out to sea, families would offer rice to the gods."

"For a good catch?"

"For a quick return." Then Daniel knew that he and Kumiko were feeling the same sadness. He considered his next words carefully.

"You ever think of coming to the States?"

"For what?"

"For dance school. For your dreams." *For mine.*

"But my whole life is here."

Daniel was startled by the familiar words. He sat down next to Kumiko on the rock, warmed by her nearness. "So you start a new one."

"Not so easy," she told him.

"The time to do it is when you're young."

"You think I would like America?"

"I think you'd love it," he assured her.

"Do you think it would love me?"

He looked at the beautiful girl next to him, touching her cheek with his finger. "I know one part of it that already does, Kumiko," he told her, leaning closer. She responded, touching his hand with hers, turning her face to his.

But before they could kiss, there was a terrible grumbling sound of heavy-duty diesel engines. Startled, Daniel and Kumiko jumped off the rock and raced out of the garden and onto the street to see what was happening. What they found was two very large bulldozers trailing a team of surveyors who were indicating which gardens were to be bulldozed to rubble.

A furious gaggle of villagers ran after the machinery, yelling and waving their arms in protest against the bulldozers. In dismay, Daniel realized that the bulldozers carried the legend SATO CONSTRUCTION.

Mr. Miyagi pushed his way through the crowd and faced the destruction team. "What are you doing?" he demanded of the lead surveyor.

From behind the man came the answer in the too-familiar voice of Sato: "I am selling the land."

"Why?" Mr. Miyagi asked, confronting Sato and Chozen.

"Why do you think?" Sato challenged.

"You will destroy the village?" Mr. Miyagi asked, incredulously.

"No, Miyagi-*san*. *You* will."

Daniel knew then that Sato had found the key to Mr. Miyagi. His friend would withstand any level of personal humiliation rather than violate his principles. But he could not ask others to withstand that same punishment for him.

"You win. I will fight," he told Sato, who sneered in victory. "On one condition."

"What?" Sato asked.

"Regardless of who wins, the deed to this land passes to the village." Mr. Miyagi would not have his friends subjected to Sato's threat a second time.

"You ask for too much."

"A small price to pay for your honor," Mr.

Miyagi told him, knowing the key to Sato.

"You are right," Sato agreed. "I will see you here. At midnight." He turned to go, but paused. "No tricks. Or this is gone," he said, indicating the whole village. "Their homes. Their school. All of it." Mr. Miyagi nodded. Sato turned to the surveyors and the bulldozers. "Leave the equipment," he told his employees, and then disappeared with Chozen, turning his back on the villagers.

Chapter 17

Daniel sat alone in the ruins of the bonsai garden that afternoon. Mr. Miyagi had wanted to be alone to contemplate, meditate, and prepare. Daniel needed to prepare as well, for the deadly confrontation was near.

Mr. Miyagi entered the garden, dressed in a formal kimono, heading for the *dojo*. He carried a scroll that he gave to Daniel, who was puzzled by it.

"Last will and testament," Mr. Miyagi explained.

The idea seemed so cold. So impossible.

"Can't you call this off?"

"Tried my best," he said.

"I don't suppose you'd consider leaving *now*, would you?"

"Daniel-*san*, don't worry."

"How can I not worry?" Daniel burst out, waving the scroll at Mr. Miyagi. "This isn't like one, two, three points, you're out. I mean, I know what happens if you lose."

"Ah, but I have already won, Daniel-*san*," Mr.

Miyagi said. "Whatever happens with Miyagi, village is saved forever." With that, he walked into the *dojo*, knelt before the family shrine, and closed his eyes in meditation.

Daniel turned his attention to the bonsai. As long as this would now belong to Yukie, not Sato, it would be repaired. He began the arduous task.

Several hours later, Yukie entered the garden, carrying a fresh-pressed karate *gi* and black belt for Mr. Miyagi.

"He's still meditating," Daniel told her.

"Hai."

"Have you seen Kumiko?" he asked, suddenly remembering that he hadn't seen her since the bulldozers had arrived. It would be at least six hours until the fight began, and he realized that he very much wanted to spend those hours with Kumiko.

"She is waiting for you," Yukie told him. "At the cannery."

Daniel brushed the dirt off himself and left Yukie to tend to Mr. Miyagi while he went to the cannery.

The cannery seemed an odd place for Kumiko to be waiting for him, but Daniel actually welcomed the walk through the village. The upcoming fight had left him feeling very hemmed in and he was enjoying the salty breeze, which seemed unusually brisk as he walked down the hill.

He passed the shrine where, on his first day in the village, he'd seen the old priest, Ichiro, teaching the children a song. Now, there was no music there. It was deserted except for Sato, who sat in motionless meditation. Behind him, Chozen knelt protectively. As Daniel passed, Chozen glanced up at him, the hatred clear in his eyes. Daniel ignored it, bent his head to the wind, and proceeded to the cannery.

He entered through the broken door, following the musical sound of wind chimes, stirred to life by the wind.

"Kumiko?" he called, but she didn't need to answer, for he had found her in the twilit room that overlooked the sea. It caught his breath to see her.

Kumiko was wearing a formal silk kimono, rich emerald green, decorated with red embroidered flowers and a red obi. Her hair was drawn up atop her head in traditional Japanese fashion, held by combs inlaid with jade flowers, just as Yukie's had been for the *cha no yu* she had prepared for Mr. Miyagi. Now, Daniel saw, Kumiko had done the same for him.

Kumiko knelt on a mat in front of a low table. Upon it were plates and bowls for the tea ceremony, as well as an exquisitely simple and beautiful flower arrangement. Kumiko greeted Daniel with a bow and indicated the pillow opposite herself for him to sit. Without speaking, he sat and watched her prepare the tea.

Gracefully, she performed the age-old ritual of tea preparation. Daniel watched in rapt silence while she mixed the boiling water with the fresh tea leaves, each intricate movement executed with such simplicity that it nearly took his breath away. Finally, blowing the steam gently from the cup, Kumiko offered it to him.

He sipped, as he had seen Mr. Miyagi do, taking only a few drops, savoring the essence of the drink and then offering it to Kumiko. She accepted, drinking as he had, looking into his eyes, her eyes shiny as diamonds, her breath shallow. Slowly, she lowered the cup from her lips and placed it on the table. Smoothly, she brought her right hand up, grasping the comb that held her hair in its formal arrangement. She removed the comb, letting her hair fall loosely to her shoulders. She moved toward Daniel. And he toward her.

As if they had all the time in the world, but none to spare, they drew closer and closer to each other, never moving their eyes from each other, nor their thoughts. Finally, their lips met and they kissed. It was as wonderful as he had hoped, and he could tell that Kumiko felt the same way he did.

Suddenly, the wind chime rattled in protest against another gust, this time much stronger than before. Kumiko pulled away from Daniel, fear in her eyes.

"What's wrong?" Daniel asked.

"Quickly," Kumiko said, in answer, gathering the tea ceremony utensils, watching the wind chime that now clacked frantically.

Daniel helped Kumiko pack the things and followed her out of the cannery. Immediately, he sensed that the wind was no longer harmless. The gale force gusts swept them up the hill, churning the waves on the sea below to foam. As suddenly as the wind had increased, the rain started, pelting down on them as they retreated.

"Does it get worse?" Daniel asked, concerned, taking Kumiko's hand and helping her climb the hill.

"Much worse," she said, dread in her voice.

Chapter 18

Almost immediately, Daniel knew that Kumiko was right. Within minutes, the gentle breeze had turned into a gusty wind and then into a gale. By the time they approached the World War II bunker that the village used for a storm shelter, the wind was ripping through the town, tugging fiercely at the trees, and whipping thatch roofs from the homes. The villagers fought against the roaring wind and the torrential rain to gain shelter. Near the shelter a bell tower stood on stilts. A young boy had scurried up the wooden ladder and was furiously ringing the bell as a warning about the storm to all who could hear.

Daniel and Kumiko met Mr. Miyagi and Yukie coming from the Miyagi house, helping Ichiro and two old women into the bunker. At the entrance, Daniel held the door against the force of the wind to allow stragglers to come in. Then he spotted a fragile old woman with an infant in her arms struggling to reach safety, unable to make headway. Quickly, he and Mr. Miyagi darted out to help them. Mr. Miyagi took the baby while Daniel guided the old woman. They bent into the wind to get back to the bunker. And just as they passed the shrine, a furious gust ripped it loose from its foundation, carrying off the roofing while the beams collapsed.

Chozen came running out from under the edge of the collapsed roof, a bloody gash on his head. He barely saw Mr. Miyagi when he ran into him, so eager was he for the comfort of the bunker.

"Where is your uncle?" Mr. Miyagi demanded.

"Dead," was all Chozen said. He fled to the bunker.

Daniel saw Mr. Miyagi look over at the shrine, in disbelief. Daniel looked at it, too. It was hard to believe Sato was actually dead — such a simple solution to such a difficult problem, and really no solution at all. But just then, another fierce blast of wind yanked at the shrine, this time tearing off a whole wall, and revealing Sato, pinned under a collapsed roof beam. The fear in his face was unmistakable. He was alive.

Without hesitation, Mr. Miyagi handed the infant to Daniel and raced to the shrine. Daniel, in turn, gave the baby to Kumiko and followed his friend.

Daniel watched as Mr. Miyagi's eyes met Sato's. But before they could speak, more of the roof collapsed onto Sato, held motionless by an ancient roof beam. Sato was certain to be crushed to death almost immediately, for the rest of the roof threatened to collapse with the next gust. Mr. Miyagi's mouth tightened as he surveyed the thick beam holding Sato prisoner. He raised his hand in a chop over his head and breathed deeply, locking his eyes onto Sato.

"This was the only way you could win," Sato said contemptuously, expecting a death blow from Mr. Miyagi.

At that instant, Mr. Miyagi brought his hand down with all his force. Involuntarily, Daniel closed his eyes.

"Kiiaiii!"

Crack!

Daniel opened his eyes. The beam that had immobilized Sato was now broken in two pieces.

"Daniel-*san*," Mr. Miyagi ordered. Quickly, Daniel came to his aid, levering the two pieces of the beam off Sato and helping the wounded man to his feet. They flanked Sato, each giving him a shoulder for support, and together they walked to the bunker.

Once inside the shelter, Kumiko and Yukie rushed to give them blankets and towels and, when he could take weight off his damaged legs, Sato bowed deeply in thanks to Mr. Miyagi.

From the rear of the bunker, Chozen came to see his uncle. Stuttering in embarrassment, he began, "I-I-I thought you were, uh, d-d-dead, Uncle. I was sure when that beam fell that there was no help for you and so I thought I should — Well, I knew you would want me to save my — And I never could have believed — What a miracle, Uncle —" He was silenced by the skeptical stare he received from Sato.

The tower bell, which had been ringing constantly since the storm had started, now began ringing frantically. Suddenly there was a loud cracking sound. The villagers crowded to the bunker's gun ports and saw, to their horror, that two of the three stilts that held the bell tower were broken. The tower tilted perilously, swaying toward some power lines. But, worst of all, the brave young boy who had been ringing the bell in warning was now swinging from the rope attached to the bell's clapper thirty feet above the ground.

Before anybody in the bunker could move, Daniel rushed out into the storm to rescue the boy.

"Help him," Sato commanded Chozen, but the fear in the young man's eyes was clear. He could not move.

Then, while Sato, Chozen, and the villagers watched, Daniel climbed the now fragile ladder of the tower to rescue the boy. When he got about halfway up, the third stilt on the tower bent sickeningly, laying the weight of the entire structure on the power lines. The lines began snapping, snaking and shooting their deadly voltage every which way in a brilliant display of electric sparks. Quickly, Daniel slipped his belt off and used it to swat at the jumping cables, just enough to keep them from hitting himself or the boy. Holding the ladder with one hand, he swung around until he could reach the frantic boy, who gratefully grabbed the offered hand and swung back to the safety of the ladder. Daniel and the boy slid down the ladder to the ground, moving away from the tower just seconds before it crashed to the ground. The two ran into the bunker together amid the joyous congratulatory cheers of the villagers.

When the cheers had quieted, Sato turned to Chozen, still standing next to him.

"You left me for dead? To you, that's what I am," he said, turning from his nephew for the final time.

Chozen was speechless. He stood motionless for a moment, then suddenly, without a word, spun on his toes and sprinted out the door into the storm.

The villagers, unaccustomed to such behavior from Sato and embarrassed by Chozen's unforgivable behavior, turned to their families, settling one another down for the long, stormy night ahead, glad for the protection of the bunker.

Chapter 19

When morning came, the wind was still, the clouds were gone, the sun shone brightly, sparkling on the ocean. In fact, it was almost hard to remember the terrible storm from the night before — except for the devastation.

The village of Tome was nearly destroyed. Uprooted trees crisscrossed the roads; roofs, walls, even floors of the fragile houses were scattered over the landscape. The precious vegetable gardens were mere mud puddles, plants and seeds carried away by the torrents of rain.

Still, with dogged determination, the villagers left the bunker at first light to begin repairs. By the time Daniel, Kumiko, Yukie, and Mr. Miyagi reached Mr. Miyagi's house, the village rang with the sounds of industry — saws to cut the felled trees, hammers to repair the broken houses. Everywhere, people were patching broken windows with cloth or wood, clearing patches of ground, preparing thatch bundles to repair roofs.

Mr. Miyagi worked near a stack of wood, pulling nails from the boards and saving them, to reuse both. Everything that could be salvaged would be used. Kumiko and Yukie worked inside the house, repairing and restoring order as best they could.

"The garden's gone," Daniel told Mr. Miyagi after reviewing the destruction behind the house. "And the seeds are all ruined." Then he noticed the boards. "You going to get enough wood that way to repair everything?"

"Doubt it," Mr. Miyagi answered truthfully.

"What are *they* going to do?" he asked about the other villagers.

"Best they can." Mr. Miyagi tugged at a stubborn nail. It gave way, springing out of the board and hitting the ground with a ping of victory. Mr. Miyagi began to work on the next nail.

But then there was another sound — the rumble of trucks. The villagers, alert to new signs of danger, looked up from their labors to see a convoy of large trucks bearing bulldozers, tractors, and end loaders, as well as hundreds of heavy-duty hand tools, and the men to use them. Each of the trucks bore the legend SATO CONSTRUCTION.

The trucks drew to a halt, and Sato's familiar black Cadillac pulled up to where Mr. Miyagi and Daniel stood. The door opened and out stepped Sato, in workman's clothes, leaning on a cane with one hand, carrying a scroll with the other. He offered the scroll to Mr. Miyagi.

"The deed to the land," he explained. "I beg your forgiveness." He bowed deeply, humbly holding the position until Mr. Miyagi touched his shoulder and took the scroll.

"There is nothing to forgive, old friend." The two men embraced each other gladly. Daniel and Kumiko could see tears of emotion forming in Mr. Miyagi's eyes.

Daniel looked at Kumiko and the other villagers and saw, for the first time, looks of real hope replace the grim defeat on their faces. Suddenly he had an idea — a way Sato could prove his friendship to Mr. Miyagi and to the people of Tome.

"Uh, Mr. Sato . . ." Daniel spoke. Sato turned to him. "You know, the Bon dance is soon and it's going to be hard to have it here in the village —"

"What are you asking of me?"

Daniel swallowed his fear and continued. "The castle," he said. "Where the dance really belongs anyway."

Sato looked at Daniel for a long time, his face revealing nothing. Then he turned to Mr. Miyagi. "Your student becomes my teacher," he said with approval, and then announced, "The *O-bon* festival will be held in the castle every year."

The villagers' cheers of joy rang through the streets until Sato spoke again.

"Under one condition," he said solemnly, facing Daniel, whose heart sank with the tone. Then Sato pointed at him: "He dances!"

Daniel's face broke into a smile. "You got it!" he promised Sato, relieved. Then he offered his hand to Sato to seal the deal American-style. Sato took it and shook it firmly.

Once the deal was made, Sato turned to the villagers and spoke to them rapidly in Japanese, explaining the reconstruction plan and putting his men and machinery to work. Quickly, the people began their tasks with renewed vigor. Now they knew that Sato would help them. He was no longer their enemy; he was their friend. As they worked to rebuild their village, they would be reconstructing their lives as well as their homes.

Chapter 20

The flames from the torches and candles danced in the soft summer night, illuminating the ancient Castle of King Shohashi. This night, it was truly the Castle of Courtesy and Good Manners, for the entire village was celebrating in joy. They were celebrating their annual *O-bon* festival honoring the dead, but they were also celebrating the repair of their village after the typhoon. And, most important, they were celebrating the return of Sato as their friend.

Sato sat with Mr. Miyagi, watching the beautiful dance on the platform in the middle of the arena, which served as a stage for the performers. With the castle under reconstruction, the only way to reach the stage was across two carefully placed boards serving as a bridge over the chasm that separated it from the audience. The stage area itself was a large circle, decorated with traditional flowers and lanterns and featuring two great stone dogs, called *fu* dogs, symbols of welcome.

On the stage, the girls of the village were dancing, dressed in their finest traditional Japanese kimonos, brilliant colors flashing in the flamelit night. Kumiko, their teacher, stood by the side, guiding them, when necessary, through the intricate, ancient dance of the festival. True to his promise to Sato, Daniel danced with them, slowly, elegantly, performing the movements Kumiko had taught him. He held a hand drum, as did the other dancers and many people in the audience. It was very similar to, though smaller than, the one in the Miyagi *dojo*. As they danced, they twirled their drums in unison, stepping to the cadence. Daniel was surprised to find himself enjoying the dance, the graceful motions being almost familiar after his study of karate.

When the music stopped and the dancers' drums ceased beating, the people of the village twirled their drums joyously, welcoming the dancers across the bridge and off the stage area so it could be clear for the evening's greatest treat. Daniel circled through the crowd and joined Mr. Miyagi and Sato to watch Kumiko dance.

Kumiko emerged from the shadows on the edge of the platform and posed, waiting for her music to start. Almost as if it were a breeze singing, the quiet strains of Ichiro's stringed instrument signaled the beginning of the dance. As if moved by the same breeze, Kumiko began. Her intricate steps were perfectly balanced by her graceful motions. Daniel could not take his eyes from this beautiful girl — nor could anyone else. The entire audience was entranced by Kumiko.

So much so that they did not see the figure dressed in black scurrying through the shadows toward the footbridge to the stage. Springing in a somersault, the figure crossed the bridge and in a single leap came up behind Kumiko, grabbing her, one arm at her waist, one at her neck. The light from the torches glinted off the shiny steel blade of the knife held at her throat.

It was Chozen.

The music faltered and stopped. The crowd gasped in realization. The two men nearest the bridge ran to Kumiko's aid, but before they could cross, Chozen spoke to them in Japanese, brandishing the knife closer still to Kumiko's throat. The rescuers stopped cold. The meaning was clear.

"Where is Daniel?" Chozen demanded.

Before Daniel could answer, Sato stood, with the aid of his cane, and spoke to his nephew. "Stop this!" he commanded.

"I cannot hear you, Uncle," Chozen taunted. "You are dead to me, remember?"

Daniel rose. "I'm here," he said.

"Cross the bridge," Chozen told him.

Daniel put down his drum and left his seat, crossing the bridge slowly, carefully, not wanting to alarm Chozen while he still held Kumiko's life in his hands.

"All right, I crossed the bridge. Now let her go."

"Over there," Chozen said, motioning Daniel away from the bridge. When Daniel stepped aside, Chozen, still holding Kumiko, moved to the edge of the makeshift bridge and kicked the boards off the edge of the stage. They clattered noisily into the chasm below. Chozen cast the knife after the boards, releasing Kumiko. She ran to Daniel. Now the three of them were completely isolated on the stage.

"What do you want?" Daniel asked.

"Revenge," was the answer.

"Everything's been settled."

"Everything but me," Chozen told him. "And I hold you responsible." Chozen circled Daniel and Kumiko and continued to speak to them, menace in his voice and step. "I have been embarrassed, humiliated, dishonored. All because of *you*."

Suddenly, Kumiko lashed out at Chozen, attacking with her fists. He grabbed her wrists as if she were no more than a rag doll, picked her up off the ground by them, and cast her aside. Her head hit the stone dog as she fell.

"Chozen!" Sato called. There was no answer.

Chozen walked toward Daniel, challenge in his step. Daniel backed up.

"Look," Daniel reasoned. "For whatever happened, I apologize."

Chozen was beyond reason. "Apology will not give me back my honor."

"Neither will this."

Chozen glanced at the villagers across the chasm. "In their eyes it will," he told Daniel.

Daniel knew that fighting Chozen was not the answer — no more than it would have been the answer for Mr. Miyagi to fight Sato. He had learned that.

"I'm not fighting," he said to Chozen.

"You're not running, either," Chozen countered. The cold truth of that sank in to Daniel. He knew he was within inches of the edge of the stage, the echoes of the boards clattering to the depths still clear in his memory. Chozen was poised in a classic karate stance only a few feet away. Behind him, the crumpled body of Kumiko lay motionless by the stone dog.

The choice was clear.

"Kiiaiiii!"

Daniel sprang at Chozen, unwinding with a kick at his ribs and finishing with a chop to his neck. Chozen blocked both attacks easily and stood, unmoving.

From the audience, Daniel heard Mr. Miyagi call to him, warning: "This is not a tournament, Daniel-*san*. This is for real."

The cold voice of Chozen echoed the thought. "Yes, for very real," he said.

That's when Daniel knew he was in a fight to the death.

Chapter 21

The realization that this was a fight to the death brought a sudden surge of energy to Daniel. Once again, he attacked, this time throwing a side kick with all his might, but once again Chozen rebuffed the attack, catching Daniel's ankle and flinging him away.

Daniel rolled, evading Chozen's follow-through stomping attack. Before Daniel could stand and attack again, however, Chozen sprang through the air at him with a flying jump, spinning over into a back kick. Evading the stunning kick, Daniel scuttled backwards, but too far.

Suddenly, there was no ground under him. Daniel slipped off the edge of the stage, grabbing the rim of the platform only at the last second. He struggled to pull himself back up, but Chozen began stomping on his fingers, slowly forcing him to release his grasp. Just as Daniel thought he would not be able to hold on any longer, he saw Kumiko, now conscious, attacking Chozen from behind.

She looped her ornamental belt, her *obi*, around

Chozen's neck and pulled as hard as she could, tugging him back from the edge of the stage, choking off his air. Chozen staggered backwards, giving Daniel the few seconds he needed to scramble up onto the stage again before Chozen overpowered Kumiko, reversing the choke, and knocking her to the ground, unconscious once again.

Daniel stepped toward Chozen, preparing to attack, but Chozen was distracted for a moment by the sound of a plank of wood landing on the edge of the stage. Several of the villagers had fetched a new bridge so they could help Daniel and Kumiko. Chozen, however, terminated their rescue efforts with the flick of a foot, which sent the new board tumbling after the old ones, clattering to the bottom of the chasm.

Chozen turned to attack Daniel again, punching fiercely. Daniel deflected the attack with the swift blocking motion he'd studied so long and knew so well. Daniel counterattacked. Chozen, in turn, blocked his attack.

Daniel spun, whipping around his opponent, snapping at the back of his head with his elbow. Chozen returned the attack, knocking Daniel against one of the stone dogs, dizzying him for a moment. While Daniel recovered, Chozen launched his next attack, jumping in the air with a flying sidekick at Daniel's face. At the last second, Daniel moved aside, as Mr. Miyagi had taught him at the cannery. Instead of hitting Daniel, Chozen struck the stone dog with such force that he broke it in half, its pieces tumbling to the ground.

Daniel came at him with a follow-up attack, striking with a kick, but Chozen grabbed Daniel's foot and threw him. Daniel hit the ground hard and before he could rise, Chozen grabbed him, pulling him to his feet from behind, and applying a death choke.

Frantically, Daniel tugged at Chozen's arm, gasping for air, but unable to break the hold. Then, the help he needed came from across the chasm.

"Step back, Daniel-*san!*" Mr. Miyagi called. "Step back. Use hips."

Yes, Daniel remembered the block with the spear. He remembered "hips for power." With a final effort, he took a step back, bracing himself with an open stance. He shifted his weight, lifting his hips. To his surprise — and Chozen's —Chozen flew straight over his head, releasing Daniel, and landing on the ground in front of him. Daniel dived at him in attack — the final attack, he hoped, for his reserves of strength were waning.

Daniel shot three punches at Chozen's chest. They seemed to take effect, knocking Chozen down, sapping his will to win. But when Daniel followed with a kick, Chozen rose at him with a devastating double-fisted punch to Daniel's face, followed by two kicks that left Daniel staggering, unable to react, near the end.

Chozen backed off from Daniel to allow room for his final attack. The crowd, which had been cheering for Daniel, was now stunned to silence.

Daniel became aware of what was happening. Weakly, he lifted his arms to defend against the death blow Chozen would deliver. Then he heard the drum. Rat-tat-tat. All eyes turned. It was Mr. Miyagi, twisting his drum back and forth. The wooden balls swung around the drum, reminding Daniel — of what? He shook his head to clear his thoughts. Then the rat-tat-tatting grew as the other villagers joined Mr. Miyagi's drumming.

The sound grew from the beat of a single drum to the cacaphony of a hundred drums. It was a message.

Chozen looked around, unsure of what to do, not understanding the meaning of the message. It wasn't for him.

Suddenly, Daniel knew what he had to do. He glanced at Mr. Miyagi, who silenced his own drum. The rest of the villagers put their drums aside. Once again, there was silence.

At that second, Chozen charged.

"KIIIAIIIIII!"

Just as he was about to crush Daniel with his lunge punch, Daniel stepped forward and twisted his body, bringing his hands up in a perfect block — just like the drum! Chozen's attack was deflected from Daniel, who struck him with the second fist, catapulting him, headfirst, against the remaining stone dog. Chozen collapsed next to the ancient symbol, the wind knocked out of him, his will receding. Then he staggered toward Daniel in a final attack.

Once again, Daniel mimicked the drum, spinning from his waist, blocking with the first hand, punching with the second. Three times, the deadly maneuver struck Chozen until he knelt on all fours, his spirit completely broken. Daniel stepped up to his opponent and, taking a handful of his hair, yanked his head up to speak to him.

"Live or die. Your choice," Daniel spat at him, knowing for the first time in his life that he could kill another person.

"Die," Chozen answered.

Nodding assent, Daniel drew his hand back, cocking it for the final attack. He remembered the feeling of the ice breaking under his power. He breathed in, deeply, focusing on the task. Before delivering the blow, he glanced at Mr. Miyagi across the bridge, seeing the look of concern in his eyes.

"Kiiiiaiiii!" Daniel yelled, firing the death blow at Chozen whose eyes closed in fear. The blow stopped short, however, with the same force that had propelled it. Chozen's eyes flicked open, surprised.

"Wrong," Daniel told him. With that, he tweaked Chozen's nose hard between his thumb and forefinger, signifying that Chozen was not worthy of an honorable death. With disdain, Daniel released Chozen, pushing him aside, and stood up, victorious.

There was a thunderous roar of cheers from the villagers and Sato. On the stage, Daniel went to Kumiko's side. She was all right, and stood carefully, with his help. He held her tenderly, looking deeply, joyously into her beautiful eyes.

Daniel glanced over at the cheering crowd, searching for his teacher, his friend. There he was. Mr. Miyagi beamed proudly back at him.

Daniel LaRusso had never felt better in his life.

Books chosen with you in mind from

point

—Pass the word.

Living...loving...growing.
That's what **POINT** books are all about!
They're books you'll love reading and
will want to tell your friends about.

Don't miss these other exciting Point titles!

NEW POINT TITLES! $2.25 each